I0665451

THE STORY OF MILK

BY DITO MONTIEL

Published by Pinchback Press
PinchbackPress.com

Cover and book design: Bonnie Barrett

Published by Pinchback Press
PinchbackPress.com

DITO MONTIEL

FOR CHARLIE

THE STORY OF MILK

WHEN THE UNIVERSE YELLS

at me, I yell right back. I say, shut up universe. Leave me alone. I'm trying to think here. Tryin' to do something with myself. Tryin' to pretend you're not dictating what I'll become, where I'll go...

You get beat down over time, though. You say, please ya know? Have a little heart. A little compassion. Stop fucking with me. You see, my heart is broken in a million pieces. Through and through and it will never be repaired... fully. Vinny's dead.

From birth, we're told by God who will break us, make us stronger, who we'll cry for at their grave and who'll mourn us at ours. Our blood: our mothers, fathers, sisters, uncles—all of them.

But on this earth strange things can happen. Sometimes magical. Especially to those of us without the bond of family: Sometimes we find our own.

For me, it was Vinny in Apartment 4D in the West Wing of the Queensbridge Projects. And, here I stand, over him. Dead. Four stories off a roof and down onto the grass that we rolled around in thrown away refrigerator boxes turned army tanks as children. He's trying to get his last words out. The last ones he'll ever say. The blood is making them almost impossible to understand. I get a little closer and put my ear to him...

MY
NAME is Jonathan White. Milk. Many years ago, I
murdered a man. I was fourteen. I shot him. I shot him
with his own gun.

You always hear people say they replay moments in
their life. I don't. Haven't. Until today. It's kinda strange
I guess how the most incredible relationship of my life
spawned from something this awful, but it did.

HANKY
WAS A
MONSTER. When deciding to write this, I had every
intention to not vilify anyone. But with Hanky, it was
impossible. He was a monster.

MY SITUATION BACK THEN was bleak.

In the housing projects with a grandmother incapable of buying food, never mind left with the responsibility of the last pale white boy here (me).

And from my translucent skin came my nickname, Milk.

MY FATHER

had been a good cop who, while suspended for being a bad one, was killed by a drug dealer.

Because of his probationary status, no one would be accountable or have to give a fuck about what he left behind (us).

"Us" became me, as my mother couldn't handle him "leaving" or the level of poverty we inherited. In her words, it was just too hard. I agreed but didn't have the option of taking off.

So there I was, left with my lost grandmother. Obese, crazy, demented? I don't know the medical term, so I'll stick with "lost."

Our misfortune landed us on the first floor of the Queensbridge Housing Projects where our window could easily be hopped up and into with the leverage of any old abandoned television, refrigerator, stove or box left on the street. And in the 80s, there seemed to be lots of them out there.

To try and imagine our apartment growing up, replace roaches with junkies then imagine a revolving door of them never leaving for your entire youth.

OUR LIVING ROOM consisted of one old television positioned on a milk crate across from a rain-soaked couch we took in off the street. A coat hanger and a few whacks to the side could get you the normal stations: 2, 4, 5, 7, 9, 11 and 13. Of course there was 47 which was in Spanish and then the free Queens version of MTV (U-68) which seemed to have some kind of deal with Weird Al Yankovich as he tirelessly ran on continuous rotation throughout my entire adolescence with funny (sort of) Michael Jackson jokes I never quite got (or liked).

On the couch were never less than two junkies smoking dust or crack and chasing it with Tango (premixed vodka and orange juice). Beside the couch were more milk crates other junkies had brought in (the only thing any of them ever brought in besides drugs and 40s) to sit on.

It seemed like the TV was never off. Days and months and years of weird *Bob Newhart, Twilight Zone* and *Partridge Family* episodes played to glassy-eyed people too old for me to be around.

If you can picture the way little kids watch cartoons, without the slightest comedic reactions to anything going on, you're getting close to the scene. Just replace Bugs Bunny with Bob Newhart and the kids with dusted unemployed 19-year-old Puerto Ricans and you're starting to head down my path. Apartment 1C.

Every once in a while, in some kind of other (outer?) worldly synchronicity, our apartment would empty out. I'd quickly lock the door and attempt to enjoy my delusion of momentary solitude.

Then came, once again, the roaches. Pouring back in through the window, unlocking the door, and repeat. I imagine this all sounds horrific, because it was. But then there was Vinny.

My best friend on the whole planet was Vincent Carter.

Vinny.

People in our projects didn't mess with me too much because I didn't really have anything anybody wanted. But occasionally we did have to at least attempt to buy groceries, which did stir trouble.

My grandmother would send me to the bulletproof Supreme Mart just outside the projects, positioned perfectly between a check cashing place and a "loose joints" candy store. No joke, it was a candy store called (in hand written letters on a cardboard sign) Loose Candy. Crazy.

I'd have a handful of food stamps, and, as I imagine cavemen did thousands of years ago in their hunt for berries, head out into the terrain.

Funny enough we actually did have broken down (sharp, rusty-edged) metal dinosaurs (we called Hepatitis Rex) outside for kids to play on.

I'd head to the Supreme Mart, and like clockwork Hanky the junkie would stop me. He'd explain how instead of two loaves of bread and peanut butter, I'd be cashing in part of my stamps for Bacardi and Night Train for him.

One day he was insisting I spend it all on him when Vinny happened to come by.

Vinny and I were the same age, but he was six feet tall and lifted weights. The leaky sand-filled kind everyone seemed to have back in the 80s.

Vinny grabbed Hanky. It completely freaked me out being we were kids and Hanky was an adult. But he threw him on the ground and told him to leave me alone.

From that day on, and throughout my childhood, we were inseparable. I hear that term used a lot these days: inseparable. But either because we were destined for each other or desperate for camaraderie, there we were, in the middle of all that craziness, together.

WHAT AN INCREDIBLEY STRANGE THING to have your story turned into a movie, but that's where, I guess, this is all going.

So let me start once again,
from the beginning...

MY NAME

IS Jonathan White. Milk. I'm pale, I'm fourteen, and it's 1986.

My building—the one I live in—is infested with crack, madness, crime, hopelessness, violence and sometimes, love.

I LIVE in the Queensbridge Housing Projects.

Apartment 1C.

I'm in my bathtub. It's cold. I've been here for hours. The water hasn't been warm for hours. My hands don't even look human anymore. I'm scared.

MANY
YEARS from now, this will be the moment.

A lot of other things will happen, but this will be the one.

It will be scripted and the actor will have no choice but to do what I'm about to.

HERE HE COMES.

Amongst all the arguing neighbors, televisions, rumblings of the underground subway busting through, I heard 19-year-old Hanky. The monster.

HANKY'D BURNT HIS FINGERTIPS

SO many times he bragged of being untraceable. He had no fingerprints left.

Whenever he came around there was that feeling you remember all your life but can only know as a kid. Proper adults would jokingly call his type a "room clearer." Problem was, it was where I lived. And he never left.

Hardly ever.

HANKY STOLE MY GRANDMOTHER'S CHECKS. He stole them and she did nothing.

We ate government cheese that arrived half stale and only got worse in our half-cold refrigerator. I hated it. No matter how hungry I was, if there was mold I could not and would not eat it.

When he stole her checks sometimes that's all we'd have. But I still wouldn't eat it. It made me sick. Maybe that's why I was so skinny.

BANG BANG

BANG. That fucking monster is bashing in my front door. That fucking Hanky.

About an hour ago I was in the hall and I had this same feeling. The one where I just wasn't gonna take it no more.

So I went to the loose broken step up toward the roof where I knew he hid his shit. I lifted the broken step and I took his gun.

That's why he's extra mad out there. Usually it's just random incoherent garbage he yells out. But this time it's clear...

"I want my gun Milk! I want my FUCKING GUN!"

EVENTUALLY he's gonna break that front door open and then he's gonna break this bathroom door open because it's made out of cheap wood and then... he's gonna find me.

And when he does, I'm gonna kill him.

I'm going to kill him with his own gun and if that's premeditated, well then, that's what's up.

BANG.
BANG.
BANG.

He's still banging the front door. I hate that sound. Flesh pounding metal. Awful.

He keeps with the banging.

I hear Vinny, Young Vicky and Chinese James out in the living room. They never leave my apartment either but that's OK. I don't hate them. They're my friends.

They keep asking me what they should do.

I don't answer.

WHAT A STUPID LITTLE KID IDEA

to hide in this bathtub. As if no one will find me. As if there are hide 'n' go seek rules with junkies looking for their missing guns.

Out in the living room I hear my friends. They're on their way to open the door. To let him in.

I wanna tell them, don't. If they do, nothing's ever gonna be the same but they don't know that. Neither did I.

The banging, though, it's what I remember best. How scary it was. How much I hated that fucker, Hanky, the more he did it.

Two hours ago we were all busy trying to write lyrics that made no sense for our ridiculous little hardcore band. Tuning un-tunable guitars, makin' hi-hats out of half-rusted pots... and now, I'm sitting in here, clenching that monsters gun.

I wanna get out and tell them not to open that door. But I know the script. It's the one I'm living.

They're gonna open that door thinking they'll get rid of him and he's gonna push right past them. Then he'll push right through this cheap wooden door and then... I'm gonna shoot that motherfucker.

TWENTY FOUR YEARS FROM NOW, a movie will be made about this

moment. The one I'm in. They just cast the kid. His name is Jake Cherry.

An actor named Channing Tatum will play the adult version. If I'm telling this story it's obvious I survived. I can't say the same for Hanky though. He won't, because I will kill him dead with his own gun that I stole from his crappy hiding space under that top step by the roof.

I'll kill him and I'll write about it and hopefully watch some actors laugh after the takes on the day they reenact it. But right now there's nothing funny about this moment. It's downright scary as shit.

I'm about to take a man's life and I imagine the moment will be with me for the rest of mine.

HERE
HE COMES.

They're yelling just like it'll say to in the script. And then... I'll do it.

The shot will be loud. Deafening. Just like in the movies. And no matter how much anyone will anticipate the moment, it should catch them off guard.

BAM! Shooting a gun is like waiting for an M-80 to go off. You can't help but squint and wait and then... bang.

But when it's being used to kill and you're fourteen it's particularly strange.

I don't mean to downplay the action, as to insinuate it's an easy thing to do. God knows, as you will by the end of this, the repercussions are eternal. I'm just trying to recall the moment.

The moment Hanky stood frozen against the crappy sheetrock wall in disbelief I'd actually done it. That I'd actually shot him.

He bent over like he had a sudden stomach cramp, revealing a blood soaked wall.

Strange, the things that stick with you. The smell of firecrackers. A smell I'd always loved, right up until that moment. I remember wondering where it was coming from and then I looked at the smoke coming out of that gun.

And then, Hanky looked at me, noticed my eyes bulging at the morbid sight, and simply said, "What?" And then it was over.

Hanky, suddenly and finally, was dead. And as quick as the fear of him harassing me and my grandmother had disappeared, the new fear of what I'd just done replaced it.

I suddenly was aware at that very moment that I would be a person with a secret. A secret forever. The kind that could ruin whatever this life hadn't.

IT'S
FUNNY, the older guys in our buildings used to play that Marvin Gaye song. The one that says, "This ain't living."

They used to say I was too young to understand it, but I did, at least that part. I'd whisper sing it over and over in my head to sleep almost every night. I used to wish I wrote it, even though those were the only words I knew.

Sure seems awfully depressing sitting here recalling that but it was strangely soothing to me...

Those words.

"This ain't living, this ain't living..."

"This ain't living, this ain't living..."

I'd sing that song to sleep and imagine being able to simply fly out my window. I'd land on the ground being we were on the first floor, but determined I'd jump once, twice and eventually... soar. Crazy dream.

Vinny used to say we dreamt of unattainable things so we'd never be let down.

He always used big words that I'd look up in the dictionary.

Unattainable: Impossible to attain; unattainable goals.

It never stopped me though. Even conscious, I'd "practice" jumping off the corner Salvation Army box hundreds and hundreds of times in a makeshift Superman outfit (towel around the neck) asking Vin to time it. Hoping, checking to see if it was taking longer for me to hit the ground with each jump.

I used to think if I could get my landing time up, just a second at a time, eventually... who knows?! I was, after all, the dreamer in this gang. If that word even applied here.

THINGS
CAN
INTERRUPT or change the course of your life; end the dreams of a child.

Murder certainly has a way of being one of those things.

Many years from that fateful day I will marry a woman named Kerry. Kerry was and is ten million miles from anything I ever knew.

"Stable" isn't the most romantic of words, but to me, it was magical. Some romantic, huh? But for me, Kerry meant my life could somehow become... OK.

We met working in a record shop in Staten Island at 19. I hesitate to say as kids because I felt my childhood had ended back in the Queensbridge Projects. But she didn't have to know that... we all have our secrets.

At 21 we made a daughter named Charolette. I like to say we made her. Makes me feel like we did something.

I hear all the time how the moment you look into your newborn's eyes your world changes. For me, this was not the case.

I spent days upon weeks upon months staring, waiting.

The same way I used to pray Jesus would come into my life, but never quite did. I needed that "moment." That burning bush. That minute believers know for certain, Jesus is their savior. That they'll live for eternity in paradise. That their newborn will now give them a true purpose in this life. But there she sat: a blob of no emotion or attention span. My daughter, Charolette.

In all truthfulness, I feared I was emotionless. A master at disguising it, I always knew the right things to say, the correct time to smile, but deep inside I feared there was nothing left.

People would compliment Charolette and I'd do the fatherly thing and agree, but it never meant anything. Until one day when she began coughing.

She coughed and coughed and then... froze. Still.

I looked at her, waiting for her to snap out of it, but it didn't happen.

Seconds became a minute until she turned blue. Next thing I knew we were rushing to a hospital where she suffered an ongoing series of Grand Mal seizures.

I prayed and prayed to the God that never came to me. Never lit that bush on fire. Never... killed Hanky for me.

I cried about the daughter I didn't understand. Made promises I didn't know if I could keep. And then, the seizures stopped.

Slowly coming out of it, she cried as her mother and I held her.

I caught myself in a hospital mirror. And saw something different. That "survivor" thing that'd inhabited me, covered me since childhood like a callusing shell of indifference was, for the first time... not there.

Kerry hugged me, unaware this was my first genuine moment with my daughter, my family. My newfound purpose. The one I'd pretended to have since her birth. Finally, the burning bush.

CHAROLETTE WAS DIAGNOSED WITH EPILEPSY.

Harrowing as that may seem, it was our bond. Had it not been for that seizure I don't know if we'd have ever connected.

We agreed on her name, Charolette, because Kerry had a grandmother with that name. In my heart it was always after my childhood dog, Charlie. I loved that dog. And before I was sure if I could ever love my daughter in the way I eventually would, I'd hoped it would make it easier.

After that seizure though, things were different.

Once she was old enough, the new Charlie in my life and I had an almost nightly ritual of imitating how my crooked old mange-ridden Charlie dog ran.

The little "blob" in my life was becoming... interesting. Someone, I don't know how to put it... that I could talk to. Someone I was falling in love with.

We'd spend hours on end about how I grew up in these huge castles (her name for the projects). She wanted to know if princesses lived in them.

It was fun and strangely peaceful to talk with her about my childhood: my dog Charlie, the buildings, my old friends. She was still young enough to divert away from any of the things I didn't want to talk about.

BACK
IN 1986 Hanky lay dead on the bathroom floor. I
looked up at his blood on the broken door hinges of my
childhood and all I felt was confusion.

People wonder how you can live with having done
a thing like this. The burden of harboring a broken
commandment; this one in particular: murder.

I thought back to something old Detective Charlie said
when I had asked that very same question through a fat
lip full of little boy tears. He simply replied, "Next time
you wonder how these people can live with what they do,
remember that even decent people often like the smell
of their own shit." Old Charlie had a way of talking to
nine year olds, a way that sort of stayed with you... if I
recall correctly. And I do.

Cold as this may sound the fear of the consequences
of being a murderer far outweighed the guilt of the
act. I believe this is probably true in many cases, for
the blood-covered walls meant nothing more at that
moment then something to cover up. Something to
clean. Something to scrub. Like they did on TV shows.
Fingerprints. Childhood pee-stained bedspreads you
don't want your mother to find, if you were lucky enough

to worry about that luxury.

All Hanky represented to anyone was a nobody no one cared about, but to me, he was someone I cared enough about to kill.

And there he was... on the bathroom floor of our undecorated, uncared for roach-infested first floor projects apartment bathroom.

My terrorist... defeated.

CHANNING TATUM will have to understand this as an actor.

We'll talk at length in this same hallway about the desperation, the regret. But, the truth is, all I can remember is the sound and that smell of firecrackers on that day. And the fear of what to do with all that blood.

Little Jonathan White in Apartment 1C. Me. Rice in a raisin box sitting in that bathtub with freezing pruned fingers holding a smoking gun. The son of no one.

THE BLOOD-SOAKED door flew open and there stood

Vinny, Young Vicky and Chinese James staring at me and Dead Hanky.

James had a joint in his mouth, which for some unexplainable reason made me feel, for just a moment, maybe, the world somehow wouldn't change. The moment didn't last.

The first great plan appropriately came from a stoned Chinese James who thought to just "flush him down the toilet. Whole!" (Hence, the argument for and against pot shall remain.) Bad "Roto Rooter" jokes ensued. Some nervous laughter and then the inevitable quiet.

The only consistent one throughout it all was Vicky. I remember just watching her. Skinny little dark skinned Vicky. Shaking almost uncontrollably. I remember being really afraid of how afraid she was. A constant reminder, besides a 200 lb. dead man on the floor, that this was some serious shit.

WHEN I
WAS
SIX YEARS OLD my father was murdered. He was a
police officer at the 118 in Queens.

No one was ever charged and just like that he was
gone. My mother took off soon after and not much was
ever said about it. That was it. I was left to the care of
my grandmother in the Queensbridge Projects.

I sometimes wonder if I'd had a seizure if that would
have changed things? If maybe that would have made
my mother change her feelings about parenthood. Like
it did, mine, with Charolette. It's funny how a "purpose"
can make "hard" things... easier?

Because my father was suspended at the time his
pension would not be paid, which I imagine made the
decision for my mother to leave that much clearer.

A one-time collection of local officers at a softball
game was made to help us out, but I was too young to
know whatever became of it. Chinese James used to
joke, it paid for the big ugly sign they put up outside the
P.A.L. league. Who knows?

My grandmother was not a bad person; she just had

no idea what to do with me. Besides being too old and poor for the job, it's my belief she was schizophrenic.

Over the years the apartment I grew up in had become somewhat communal grounds for the misplaced. And the misplaced members of 1980s Queensbridge Projects were a tough crowd.

It was somewhat second nature to me. Not the kind that's good for you, just the kind you adjust to.

I'd use, "if you can't beat 'em, join 'em" to explain the junkies who never left my apartment, but that wouldn't do it—the truth was, you can't beat 'em and you have no choice but to be joined ... at the hip... in your living room. Eating the little food you had in your refrigerator.

Fuck 'em. I hated the stale Government cheese anyway.

Hanky was a different breed though, even from them.

Everyone was afraid of him. I'm not even sure that breed exists anymore. That breed of dungaree sleeves-cut-off nomad, aimless, half-a-gang Puerto Ricans, who roamed New York's 1980s projects looking to simply scare people.

Sometimes I wondered if he even knew how scary he was. But then I came to the thought that he really liked the power he held—even if it was just over little kids and occasional old ladies.

Since I left that world many years ago it sometimes feels like a long extended TV show I watched but wasn't in. The kind where the mystery isn't solved.

I wonder if it's still like that there, or anywhere. The world seems so much different now.

But then again, it's been a long time since I've been in that world.

MY WORLD
THESE
DAYS is quiet, somewhat boring. Suburbia. The kind
of place I'd always dreamed about.

   We live in Staten Island: me, Kerry and Charolette.
My past buried somewhere deep in the quiet of that
forbidden memory. Deep amongst the secrets of a
corrupt police station.

DETECTIVE CHARLIE STANFORD was older than someone you'd expect

to be coming around questioning who killed some junkie no one cared about (if, of course, you think about these things). Grandfatherly would probably best describe him.

He had been my father's partner back in the 1970s, which in New York was the equivalent to the Wild West. I heard some guy on TV once say, every time you question the violence of New York's 1980s, refer to the 70s first.

When my father was murdered, Detective Charlie would come almost nightly, after his shift, bringing food he didn't finish from the diner.

I can still remember the smell of thick cut pork chops, left at my window from the Neptune Diner near his precinct. He'd leave what he didn't finish by my window as he knew if he left them at my door the junkies would get them.

I felt it was his way of saying, "Don't worry kid, someone's still out here." Someone who didn't finish his pork chops. Ha.

Well, he did take the time to bring the leftovers so I should be thankful. And as a kid, I was.

Occasionally he'd come in for a quick evacuation of the vagrants. It'd last until about one minute after he left but it never stopped me from hoping this was the time they wouldn't return.

Detective Charlie hated all the junkies.

At first they'd run at the sight of him. But like overused antibiotics or roach spray, eventually immunity to anything begins to build and they barely even got up.

He hated every one of them.

And to him, "them" meant simply... "them." As in all of them. Every last one... Vinny included.

Basically, Detective Charlie would preach "if you're friends with one, you're friends with them all." I used to listen to him about everything, but not this, at least not while we were kids. Because without Vinny, I would have had no one.

ON MY THIRTIETH BIRTHDAY, many years and miles from that place, I

became a police officer. Kinda funny to start a career like that so late, but your options are limited with a G.E.D. and when looking for health insurance for your family, especially when you have a daughter in need of frequent medical attention.

Six days after I graduated the academy, the Twin Towers were toppled by terrorists.

New York and the rest of the country were in dismay, which led to something no one could have foreseen: warmth.

For the next six months there was a feeling of camaraderie in New York. Everywhere you went there were American flags hanging. People being friendly. It felt inexplicably good.

It was as if everyone's values were back in order again. All the greed ridden thought process instilled from the 80s and tech heads of the 90s had somehow temporarily vanished in the smoke of those buildings coming down.

Little kids waved at firemen. Standing for the national anthem no longer felt like an obligation, but a desire. The plea of a young boy wanting to be a police officer was no longer met with the tales of crappy pay we all got, but the good he could do. It was as if America was thrown into a 1950s time warp.

It felt like nothing this good could last ... and nothing did.

Within six months questions started to arise. And along with questions came concerns which inevitably led to skepticism. And slowly but surely, the love affair between the public and authority was ending.

The first time I came into the station and saw the endless row of lit candles by the curb vandalized, I knew something was different. Nothing too dramatic. Just knocked over. But the fact no one picked them up by the end of day spoke lots. That 50s feeling was dissipating. Things were changing.

JUST AS I WAS SETTLING IN

to my job at the local 122nd precinct in Staten Island, where not much happened aside from the local drunks, I was notified I would be transferred to the 118 in Queens. The station seven blocks from where I'd grown up.

Supposedly there was something going on there called the "Quality Of Life," sweeps, and they needed more men.

This isn't all that strange when you're a rookie. The idea of being transferred. But being transferred back to the neighborhood you grew up in; more precisely the station in charge of the neighborhood I'd committed murder in, certainly was unsettling.

And there I was... back.

THE PARTNER
I WAS
ASSIGNED TO
WAS Officer Thomas Prudenti. A good-looking,

hard-to-figure guy with a long and precise take on
conspiracy theories.

Prudenti, in many ways, was not what you would
expect your average cop to be. Certainly not part of
any sort of brotherhood. I'd use "complex" but that
would be undermining him.

One part, "don't ask, don't tell," the other, extremely
skeptical of the first part.

Day in and day out we'd spend long hours checking
in on the same old cases. Mr. Winters complaining the
people upstairs (he lived on the top floor) were shooting
guns. A few petty car break-ins and the occasional family
disturbance. "Bullshit" as he'd put it.

My old neighborhood was somewhat gentrified at
this point. The crime I grew up with had made way for
Starbucks and Gaps. Funny, hearing Yuppies complaining
how it was becoming gentrified. Such is life. Ironic.

Long hours, side by side in our squad car with Prudenti preaching, "twenty in, twenty out" as in, "just keep a low profile and you can retire in twenty years." Crazy to think of the wide scope his seemingly narrow view had.

The doldrums of endless hours in an "unwanted gasoline box with a bullseye on it" (his term for our car) spawned strange conversational time-passing games. His favorite being "What Would You Do?" A little game he invented based on what levels we'd go to for a million dollars.

I'd try and play along with the obvious, "lose a pinky?" As he'd always diabolically steer it to what seemed like overly-thought-out warrants for police therapy. "Kill someone you liked (but didn't love) if there was no way of them tracing it to you!"

On the lighter side he'd drop things like "have a pebble in your shoe you never get used to" but more often it was the well-thought-out-diabolical.

On our drives, one street in particular always had him bothered.

Steinway Street was a one block stretch of Mosques, hookah stores and Middle Eastern cafes. There was literally a store called "Read the Koran." A far cry from the Guido-ridden street I'd remembered as a kid, where

Italians boasted gold crosses and *Kiss Me I'm Italian* T's
while huge ITALIA/AMERICA flags swayed in the summer
wind to Sinatra.

According to Prudenti, and quite a few at the 118,
the people here were "dancing in the streets" on
September 11th. "Happy as pigs in shit over the towers
coming down."

He hated these fuckers and I could understand.
The whole city was going through a very hard and
strange time.

ON CHRISTMAS EVE

2001 I was assigned to be part of the seventh in a series of the "Quality Of Life" sweeps at my old projects. No one at the precinct understood this to be my old neighborhood. Who would? Pale as a ghost, it was pretty much a hundred percent African American, even back then.

What a strange way to return to your childhood home though. As a cop. In a raid.

We were told to be harsh, and if necessary, brutal.

Anyone and everyone who even looked cross should be brought in. And knowing the cops who were going to determine who looked "cross," I imagined correctly that we were going to need a lot of holding space. Paddy wagons.

The idea of doing this on Christmas Eve didn't even dawn on me until I saw the Christmas wrapping paper-covered doors inside. A tradition since before even I was a kid there.

Christmas or not, we were told this was for the good of the people, and we were there to round up everyone in question of being on the wrong side of us, the law.

At the academy, you study so much law, you can't help but question orders like those. But the memory of what it was like growing up in those projects helped me justify it all. God, how I wished something like this had been done when I was a kid. Taken them all in. Every last one of them.

Thomas Jefferson said, "Better one hundred guilty men go free than one innocent man be condemned." But I'm here to say that fucker didn't grow up in my building. At least not in the 1980s because I'd have taken those numbers any day.

Still, as an adult, now, it all didn't feel right.

ONE HAPPY CHRISTMAS

there was a guy we called "Booker"— named after the 'super' on the TV show *Good Times*.

On that Christmas Eve (supposedly on immense amounts of Angel Dust) he broke into the local store (Genovese), and when I say broke in I mean, drove a stolen pickup truck through the front window.

He threw everything he could fit onto the back of that truck, put on a Santa Claus hat and parked it right in the middle basketball court of our projects blasting Public Enemy's "Don't Believe The Hype" as we all rummaged through "free" microwaves, school books, Elmer's Glue's and random junk toys. Christmas in Queensbridge, 1986.

By the time the police came I don't believe there were even doors left on the truck. Everything was gone. A happy Christmas.

But this was many years from Booker, and I had a job to do.

AS WE CRAMMED TOO MANY LOCALS

into a makeshift paddy wagon I looked up and could swear I saw Vicky. Young Vicky, now older. There she was, looking out her third floor window at me as I pushed my old neighbors into a police bus.

Sellout. Traitor. Cop. Christmas.

When I returned that night from the raid I met Captain Marion Mathers for the first time. I'd been briefed on him. A no-nonsense, lifer cop headed for some supposed promotion. Prudenti regarded him in his usual hot and cold way. It seemed in one way he admired what a bad ass he could be, and on the other, hated him for it.

I had no idea how deep a hole I was about to be returned to. But it was to begin, again, here.

I WAS AT MY LOCKER WHEN IT HAPPENED.

Alone.

Mathers walked in and asked if I enjoyed my job in a way you just know something's up.

I said I was up for whatever they asked.

That seemed to pique his interest. He stared at me for what seemed like an eternity. Then questioned what I meant by, "whatever?" I uncomfortably half laughed and said I was there to do my job. He smiled again, stared again, and threw a paper down on my bench as he left. "Here, if you get bored, take a look." He took a beat, looked right at me. "As a matter of fact, definitely take a look."

And he left.

I looked down at a local free supermarket rag called *The Queens Gazette.* The kind of paper full of local stories no one gives a damn about. Senior citizens at dance recitals, 50th year restaurant anniversaries, church garage sales. Local crap.

I didn't think much of it. I was very wrong. This was the

beginning of the scariest turn of events in my life.
Aside from the murders.

IN 1986 I sat in that bathtub covered in Hanky's blood for what must had been an hour surrounded by a bunch of fellow fourteen year olds trying to figure it out.

Chinese James, Young Vicky and Vinny spent most of it reassuring me how it was the right thing to have done.

Among other things, years earlier Hanky'd slapped Vicky so hard she'd lost a baby tooth, threw James' mother down a flight of stairs and was, up until his death, stealing my grandmother's checks. We convinced ourselves (or momentarily pretended to) that there had been no alternative. That not only was this the only way life could return to normal but that somehow it would.

Either way, there was a 200 lb. dead man in my bathroom; I was covered in his blood with his gun literally smoking in my hands.

Suddenly there was another bang on the front door. Startled, I dropped it to the ground. Into Hanky's blood.

James turned.

"Don't answer it!" I gasped.

I looked down at my scrawny legs, shaking uncontrollably.

In that instant Geronimo made his way in.

Geronimo was one of many local dealers. Scraping two

dollar profits by crushing and mixing low-grade cocaine with blackboard chalk and selling it to the zombies that never left my living room.

As Geronimo entered, Vinny turned to me. "Pretend like you're taking a bath in here!"

He slammed the broken hinged door closed, and headed to ward him off.

I could hear the commotion as I scrambled to lift Dead Hanky into the bathtub. Not thinking I was leaving a lifetime of blood everywhere. I was convinced if Geronimo did find his way into the bathroom, I could hide behind the shower curtain with the dead body and maybe he wouldn't notice. The things kids can think.

Dead Hanky felt like he weighed a thousand pounds. The blood was everywhere. At one point I almost choked trying to lift him as his mouth opened and about a gallon of some yellowish drool poured directly into mine. The taste was indescribable.

I spit it out all over his face. All over that junkie's face. The mother fucker who made me do this. Made me fucking kill him.

AND THEN THERE WAS ANOTHER BANG.

Geronimo was now at my bathroom door.

Vinny, James and Young Vicky stared helplessly as he pushed his way in. He turned back to them, wondering what happened to the hinges, but he was much more interested in getting to that toilet.

He'd been to White Castle and the "murder burgers" as we called them (25 cents each for mystery meat) were being rejected by his anemic junkie shit body.

Bam! Through the bathroom door he came. Nature's calling by way of White Castle. Straight to that toilet.

Somehow I made it behind the shower curtain. Me and dead Hanky. I could hear that disgusting pig devouring that toilet, relishing in it, as I sat two feet from him in a bathtub full of dead junkie, separated by a 99 cent shower curtain.

I decided, the minute that piece of shit opened the curtain I'd blow him away too. Kill him. Fuck it, nothing left to lose.

But I needed my gun and it wasn't there.

It had to be here somewhere in that bathtub. Had to be! But the blood was everywhere.

Through the curtain, Geronimo asked what I was doing in the bathtub.

"Taking a bath!"

With a snarl he laughed, "Yeah, you can use a bath."

I was confused as to why he wasn't questioning the blood splattered everywhere.

But then I remembered, these fuckers wouldn't notice a room full of splattered blood if they were sitting in it. Taking a shit.

"Don't look in here!" I yelled.

"Fuck wants to see your transparent pecker?" He answered half to himself, the way junkies always seem to.

I scrambled some more for the gun. I thought, maybe it was under Hanky. So I reached under him as my hand accidentally inserted itself into his open wound! My God! I pulled it out as it took everything I had not to scream at the heinousness of it all. But I didn't. I stayed silent. Disgusted, terrified, angry and wondering... where the fuck was the gun?

And then, through the shadow of the curtain I watched

Geronimo reach into a puddle of Hanky's blood and pick the gun up out of it. Right where I'd dropped it.

Shit!

He took it, and without a word, left.

He had it: the evidence, the weapon. The thing that could ruin me. The actual "smoking gun."

The only solace I could find, if any, was the fact the gun was probably worth about a hundred dollars and knowing how hard up Geronomio was, I hoped he'd try and hock it.

BACK AT THE POLICE STATION

locker room in 2001 I looked at that paper. The one Captain Mathers had left for me. *The Queens Gazette.* It was folded to a page.

A handwritten letter to a reporter named Loren Bridges, printed on the page read:

> *Reporter Bridges,*
> *In 1986 two people were killed in*
> *the Queensbridge projects. The 118*
> *investigated. No one was arrested.*
> *I cared and still do. How about you?*
> *—MDC*

I couldn't stop staring at it. Through it. The single most terrifying thing I'd ever laid eyes on.

My mind was racing. Like a rolodex of everyone and everything I'd ever known. MDC?

Every move I'd ever made. Every step in my life, up until that moment.

What did it mean? Who was writing this? Why did

Mathers hand it to me? Who was MDC? And why did those initials ring a strange distant bell?

I had nothing but questions. None were good.

Halfway between Queens and my new life in Staten Island I sat in a big empty Home Depot parking lot off the Verrazano Bridge: me, some orange neon, the rain pattering off my parked windshield, and *The Gazette*.

I read and reread the letter. The way a twelve-year-old does an F on a report card, trying to figure some master scheme to hide it. Make it disappear.

Strangely, the reporter, Loren Bridges, had no article below it. Nothing.

She'd simply printed the abstract letter.

Typical of some random, unedited local paper. I could only hope they would continue to treat this so carelessly.

The fact the police Captain at the station I was "randomly" transferred to had handed it to me made me think, realize, it probably wouldn't disappear, It also started me wondering just how random my transfer had been.

BACK
IN
THAT
BATHROOM in 1986, I sat again with that same

helpless gaze.

Geronimo was gone. Gone with the gun. Would he really hock it? Would he go to the cops? Blackmail us? How could he? We didn't have anything!

Vinny said not to worry. Vinny always said not to worry.

He was sure Geronimo would hock it and get whatever crappy price he could off the streets for it. That he'd be doing our dirty work for us.

All we had to figure was what to do with Hanky's body and we'd be OK.

Later, under the cover of projects night, the four of us: me, Vinny, Young Vicky and Chinese James, stuffed Dead Hanky in an A&P grocery shopping cart and proceeded to make it about three hundred feet out the door before getting nervous and dumping him in the trash.

And there he was, just like that... garbage. James even took a moment to joke how an old *New York Post* headline, that randomly and coincidentally stuck to him, read "Can someone please clean up this city!" Referring to the garbage strike going on at the moment.

I remember staying up all night hoping the scabbing garbage men would come and take him away. They never noticed much of anything anyway.

Half delirious from no sleep, me and Vinny sat in Vicky's hallway just waiting. She had the only view of the garbage and would come tell us if anything was happening. Not that it would help but as I mentioned before… kids' heads.

Around 6 a.m. we heard that sound: the backing up ringing of a garbage truck. To this day, that beeping, like an old lover's perfume or favorite song, brings me to that exact moment.

And then, the beeping stopped.

One hour later there were three police cars and an ambulance outside. Not exactly the cavalry but then again, who cared?

Just another dead nobody in the projects, I'd hoped.

Chinese James was fast asleep when Young Vicky came running down the hall with the report.

The cops had found the body and Detective Charlie was walking into our building.

My heart literally sank. I looked around but saw nothing. Momentary nervous blindness I imagine—if there is such a thing.

Vinny, as always, said not to worry as I ran back to my apartment and hid. What a ridiculous thought. To hide. Kids shit.

For the first time, in as long as I could remember, no one was there, except, of course Chonga (as burnt as a burnout can be), but it didn't matter, all he ever did was sleep.

I remember coming in as my dog Charlie tried to get out (the routine). Before I could figure how to pretend to look comfortable, a knock came on my door.

It was Al Pacino.

AL PACINO plays the role of Detective Charlie in the movie. I remember sitting outside these same projects one day as he looked out at all the extras. There were about 50 kids dressed like it was the 80s, playing on metal clamp skates, worn in NY Knicks gas station basketballs, Klick Klacks and other random old 80s toys.

I heard him say he wished every kid could grow up in a place like this.

I looked to see if he was joking. He wasn't. Truth is, this was no place for a child when I was growing up.

After about an hour everybody went inside to a double apartment. Not my old one, same shared courtyard though. Word around here is that it was the basketball player, Ron Artest's old apartment, "Ron Ron."

I ate some of the free food they had and then, the movie cameras went up. And word for word I got to watch the greatest living actor say and do exactly what Detective Charlie said and did to me all those years ago.

He took his time, just like I'd remembered. No direction to do it. Seemed to just come instinctually.

He looked at the broken door, then the broken hinges on the bathroom that the actor playing Hanky caused, and said nothing. Just looked at them and then me. Making sure I knew that he had taken notice.

I took a moment. Was that in the script? That Al Pacino would look off camera (not at the actor but to ME)? And then, just like that... there I was again, Milk, back in 1986 in those dirty projects again.

DETECTIVE
CHARLIE STANFORD looked, for what felt like

an hour, right through me. He then asked that we walk outside. We walked through the graffiti, drug-stained walls of my hallway, on through to outside. He sat me on a bench right in the middle of everything and everyone. We were less than 100 feet from where Dead Hanky was finally being removed and said nothing about it. It took everything I had not to look either.

Detective Charlie proceeded to talk in circles about what a good man my father was. How tough it must have been to grow up in a place like this. How he knew of my grandmother's shortcomings and how one day I'd be far away from this place. How, on that day, the people here would mean nothing, and how I couldn't waste my life protecting any of them now.

As an adult now I know what he was doing. At 14 I was preoccupied with who was watching me from behind the hundreds of window curtains swaying in the wind.

"This is simply a moment you're in, Jonathan. Don't let it define you... mess with the millions you'll have in this life."

He took an overly exaggerated moment on that last part. Then went on... He asked if I understood what the police and ambulance workers to the right of me were doing. I said I didn't. We both knew that wasn't true.

I look back now and believe he was trying to scare me. Trying to make me think whoever I was protecting would see me out there with him, making it look like I'd ratted them out.

Of course this would have been more effective if I hadn't been the killer myself.

Hard to say those words even now. But I was a murderer at 14 and it wouldn't stop there.

EXT. PROJECTS - BENCHES
Detective Charlie Stanford walks Milk outside. They stop at the concrete chess table bench, in plain sight of everyone.

DETECTIVE CHARLIE STANFORD
Why don't we sit right here Jonathan. That OK with you? What a pretty day, huh? Squirrels out. What more could you want?

They sit less than 100 feet from the CRIME SCENE.

> **DETECTIVE CHARLIE STANFORD**
> **(CONT'D)**
> You seem a little shaken up. Is
> there a reason for that?

Milk barely shrugs.

> **DETECTIVE CHARLIE STANFORD**
> **(CONT'D)**
> That's a nice grandmother you got
> there. A lot a kids around here'd
> be a lot better off if they had
> one of those in their life. Do you
> know what a gift that is? What a
> blessing that is in this world?

Milk looks at the surrounding buildings, then back
down.

> **DETECTIVE CHARLIE STANFORD**
> **(CONT'D)**
> It isn't easy growing up around

here is it, Jonathan? Especially
without a father. And he was a good
man, your father.

No answer.

>   **DETECTIVE CHARLIE STANFORD**
>   **(CONT'D)**
> I know what happens when you
> try and take your little dog for
> a walk. Least thing God could
> have done is given you a little
> pigmentation, a little color before
> throwing you into all this...

Milk looks up as a curtain blows in the wind.

>   **DETECTIVE CHARLIE STANFORD**
>   **(CONT'D)**
> I first used to come here after your
> father passed, I was your escort
> home, remember? Your grandmother'd
> send you for a carton of eggs,
> you'd come home with them smashed

all over your face. Crying.

        MILK
I'm gonna go in OK?

Stanford's not done yet.

        DETECTIVE CHARLIE STANFORD
I try and talk with the people
around here, nobody knows anything.

Another random curtain moves.

        DETECTIVE CHARLIE STANFORD
        (CONT'D)
You know why you're here, don't
you? With all of them (the windows)
wondering what Detective Charlie...
white Officer Charlie's talking with
little white Jonathan about? But a
few are particularly concerned. You
know why that is? Why a few of them
might be concerned you might know
something about some dead junkie

last seen pushing through your door
there? Ending up, 200 feet from
that same door?

No answer as Milk and Stanford look at the body.

> **DETECTIVE CHARLIE STANFORD**
> **(CONT'D)**
> You don't know why that is huh?
> You're a deer in the jungle here,
> my boy, and that Hanky wasn't worth
> two damn cents, Milk.

Milk looks at Detective Stanford.

> **DETECTIVE CHARLIE STANFORD**
> **(CONT'D)**
> That's what they call you, right?
> Milk. Not a single one worth two
> cents, never mind the rest of
> your youth and you got a lot of
> that left. You understand what I'm
> saying? What I'm trying to tell
> you? I want you to look at me.

Milk doesn't. Milk and Stanford look at the body.

> **MILK**
> I'm looking at you.

                    DETECTIVE CHARLIE STANFORD
        I said I want you to look at me.

Milk forces a look.

                    DETECTIVE CHARLIE STANFORD
                    (CONT'D)
        OK then. Now you can go. But you
        hear something about that waste of
        life getting killed you come talk
        to Officer Charlie about it. You
        hear what I'm saying? I want you to
        say yes.

Milk gets away with as small a "yes" as he can get
away with and hesitantly gets up.

                    DETECTIVE CHARLIE STANFORD
                    (CONT'D)
        OK.

Milk walks back towards the building as he notices
Young Vicky watching from her window. They stay on
each other. Vicky then looks at Detective Stanford, he
looks back at her and she continues to stare.

I WENT HOME AND HELD MY DOG

Charlie for what must have been an hour after that. Poor thing was probably wondering what he'd finally done right. Like a good dog though, he stayed right there. And aside from Vinny, no one else ever would be there for me like that, not until I met my wife, Kerry.

I WAS ALREADY AT LEAST AN HOUR LATE GETTING HOME

but all I could do was sit frozen in that huge abandoned Home Depot parking lot reading and rereading that article. The thing I feared more than anything else in the world. The thing I knew eventually had to surface.

I could see the Verrazano Bridge right over there. The thing that used to signify a goodbye to all that past I had. Now it stood there simply as a reminder as to how much I had to lose.

I tried to convince myself that maybe the article was about someone else. After all, there had to be lots of unsolved murders back in 1986. In Queensbridge. Unsolved. That the 118 investigated. Little by little it just kept summoning doom.

And in all honesty, all I could really think about was Kerry and Charlie.

I was actually more afraid of how Kerry would react to the fact I never told her than the consequences from the law. But that's what love can do for or to you I guess.

I GOT BACK TO STATEN ISLAND

around 10 p.m. Pretty late as my days ended at 6 p.m. Of course, being a cop, there's always a good excuse for running late. A cop is a strange life. Scattered, unpredictable and then, strangely, routine.

Like clockwork I'll arrive and little Charlie will try to scare me at the door. Kerry will wonder why I'm late. Charlie and I will do our nightly sleep time ritual and I'll retire to my wife in bed.

What may sound simple, plain, mundane, or downright bland to some people, to me was bliss. Normalcy. All I ever dreamt of. And now it was in jeopardy.

The thought of prison can easily be trivialized in movies or on TV. People'll talk about doing five years "standing on their head." As if it were something you just sucked up and "dealt with."

For me it's the fear of losing everything. Not the violence or segregation from society, or the loss of freedom, but of the unknown. I mean, how do I know who will be left when I get out? Where will everyone be?

Where would Kerry and Charlie be?

MY NIGHT BESIDE KERRY

played out like most nights beside her. I'll pretend to be asleep long enough for her to follow and then I'll retreat downstairs. This had just become the way I dealt with my past.

I walked down the creaky steps. And suddenly everything had meaning. The thought of a second floor in my house. My house. A house with two floors. A family. Mine!

No hallway full of people. No apartment full of people.

I hadn't even thought of them since I left them back there. Back in Queensbridge. All those years ago. And now they were consuming me. All those faces that never left me alone back then. Never let me just be... a kid with a dog.

DOWNSTAIRS I stared and stared at the letter in that crappy newspaper. Trying to make sense of it.

To be sure I was alone I cautiously glanced over my head before reading the letter again.

> *Reporter Bridges,*
> *In 1986 two people were killed in*
> *the Queensbridge projects. The 118*
> *investigated. No one was arrested.*
> *I cared and still do. How about you?*
> *—MDC*

Once again, MDC. What was it about those initials? I went online and Googled "MDC." And there it was.

When we were kids, before everything was a Google away, Vinny found a record lying on the curb. We took it and rushed it home. I had a sort of snap case box looking thing that opened and became a record player. We were intrigued with the name of the band: Millions of Dead Cops. And their logo: MDC.

The music was so fast and loud we couldn't understand anything the guy was saying but this was when bands were nice enough to include their words on the sleeve.

We followed the lyrics until we could sing along. It was one of my best memories. Us screaming along with the words to "Dead Cops" and "John Wayne Was a Nazi." We didn't have any idea what they meant, but we loved it.

So here I am. Now. A thirty-year-old father in suburbia looking at a website for the band Millions of Dead Cops, beside a letter to a local paper. Dreading my past, worrying about the future.

The song "Dead Cops" is blaring from the page:

> Dead cops
> Down on the street
> Giving poor the heat
> With their clubs and guns
> Doin' it all for fun
> Dead Cops
> Big bad and blue
> They're in the Klan too
> Brutality is their sport
> We'll put 'em to the torch
> Dead Cops

It's all starting to make sense. The letter. The concern. The confession. The signature.

If my childhood friend, Vinny, is writing these letters,

if the guilt I managed to sweep away for all these years has overtaken him, we're in serious trouble. Or I'm very soon to be.

Why though? Does he hate cops? Does he know I became one? Is he trying to get back at me for leaving the neighborhood? I had no choice. I was fourteen. And by the grace of God an aunt I barely knew took me in.

Over the years since Hanky, I've found fifty ways to privately justify why I'd done what I'd done. Why I moved on and pretended it and everyone I knew never existed. And the only thing I never did find a way to feel right about was leaving Vinny. Vinny was my friend. And I never did take those words lightly.

As an adult you can make a lot of friends, but back then I had one: him.

He was simply... everything. Every once in a private while I'll take a moment to try to touch that place to find the words to explain what a person like that could mean but I simply cannot.

It's too long ago, too distant. Too much has happened since. Life has deluded the meaning. But the fact I still search for those words gives me at least an inkling how lucky I was that he had been there.

IT'S NOT
FAIR. This diluting of things. Memories... feelings.

I guess without it we couldn't go on. But something just doesn't seem fair about them all just watering down to meaninglessness.

The fact someone can mean so much and then time steps in and... it all just becomes... kid stuff.

Last I saw Vinny I'd left him back there, in hell. The more I thought about it, the more I couldn't blame him for wanting to take me down, if that was his intention with these letters. If, in fact, he was the one writing them.

His mother had a boyfriend who was a monster. The things Vinny said he'd done to him as a child were "projects bad." That was a term we jokingly used for the level of stuff we experienced.

I remember a comedian once defining rich in different levels. There's "nice car" money, "nice house" money and then there's Michael Jackson rich which he called "giraffe money." When you own a giraffe that's a whole different shit. Giraffe money! Ha.

"Projects bad" was our term.

Funny how young we were back then, but always talked about our "youth" as if it were some distant past.

In our buildings, it seemed, once you stopped getting off on seesaws you were no longer a kid.

Vinny's mother's boyfriend would molest him on an almost daily basis.

Vinny'd convinced himself his mother didn't know it was going on but how could that be? We all lived in the closest of quarters. I knew what was going on and I was four floors below them.

Every time Vinny threatened to expose him he'd be met with the threat of being sent back to that hospital. Elmwood Youth Psychiatric. That fucking hospital.

Paintings of chickens and balloons all over the walls, but we knew what it was. No kid had any business being there. Ever.

Suburban kids or kids with decent homes would go away to places like camp. When our parents couldn't handle us, or needed a "break" Elmwood was the place.

The good and bad part of welfare was once you got it, it wasn't all that hard to get thrown into one of those places. It was like a city paid vacation for parents, except instead of swimming and hiking the kids are all hopped down on Thorazine and propped up in front of

The Bob Newhart Show reruns. That fucking show.

All you needed was a parent caring enough to put in enough effort to neglectfully incarcerate you. Then the government would do their thing.

They'd ask a few questions you couldn't possibly answer well enough, and the next you knew they're pumping as many cc's as they could legally administer into you.

I guess you can say I was lucky to have a grandmother so out of it she couldn't even muster the effort to put me into one of those places. I imagine it also took a certain amount of downright meanness to do that. And, like I said, she wasn't mean, just out of it.

Poor Vinny though, that hospital was almost a yearly thing and we hadn't lived enough years for that.

As a kid I was always afraid to visit him because I thought... what if they didn't let me leave? After all, he wasn't any crazier than me. I'd even heard and believed there were actual zombies in there. That's just how young and messed up we all were.

But the last time I saw him, he was in there. In that hell. And I'm here to confirm, surrounded by zombies.

I SHOWED UP TO VISIT VINNY

with my 14-year-old ID card and walked right on up to the adult psychiatric ward where they were holding him.

Seems all the children's wards were booked up and because no one checked up (or cared) about Vinny they squeezed him in with the adults. Hey, welfare is welfare and I'm sure there was a buck to be made somewhere. A seat to be filled.

I always wondered if the people who made those decisions had any idea what the repercussions were. I can't imagine they'd have made them if they did. I still believe humans have to be inherently good.

I got to the visiting room and picked a table where no one was drooling. Away from the zombies.

The place stunk worse than our projects' pissed-in elevators.

I sat waiting for my friend, and then he came.

My protector. The only person I'd ever felt safe around,

shuffling his feet across the yellow stained tiles like a ninety-year-old man.

His hair was all messed up. White shit on the side of his mouth.

I'd like to say it made me feel sad but the selfish truth was that was the moment I knew I had to get away. That there was no one left. That survivor shit that can make you just that much less... decent.

He sat and with every last bit of strength, through all the medication, managed to squeeze out the words to let me know, he'd never tell anyone. No matter what.

"I'll never tell anyone, Milk. Ever. I'll never let them get to you."

And there he was, still worried about me. My real superhero. My protector.

And again, this should have been the moment I felt that compassion, that camaraderie, but the change in me had already begun. All his actions meant at that moment was that he was weaker than me. And I was already weak enough.

On my way home, on the 7 train, I thought of a sermon I'd heard once in a Mass where the priest said he wanted "a strong God." The type that "picked you up when you were down."

I guess I'd always looked to Vinny in a Godly way. And this was my out. Yeah, I needed a strong God. And he was weak.

This was to be my out. I was to become, in a biblical way, Peter, and deny him. A rat on a sinking ship.

BACK, TODAY, SITTING

in the safety of years gone by and my new life in Staten Island, I was so entranced with these long compartmentalized memories of betraying Vinny, I hadn't realized the song "Dead Cops" on the MDC web page was playing until suddenly, my daughter Charlie tapped me on the shoulder.

I jumped and quickly clicked off the page before she could see the images of police beating people. Photoshopped photos changing riot gear to Ku Klux Klan hoods.

"What are you doing up Charlie?" I asked. When the real question should have been, what was I doing up?

She rubbed her sleepy eyes as I carried her up to bed. Later on, just like in the movies, the three of us lay quietly in bed together. Father, mother and daughter.

I remember thinking how these were the times I'd dreamed about. These were the moments to "be" in. But my present at this moment had no choice but to dabble in both my past and my future.

THE NEXT MORNING I walked into the 118 in the midst of madness.

There'd just been another "Quality Of Life" sweep in the projects and it seemed half the neighborhood had been arrested.

I met eyes with a Puerto Rican teenager in half ghetto drag asking why it was a crime to "sit in my own fucking hallway!"

I held his gaze for half a moment before shamefully moving on.

I'd been told a local developer had been looking into a way to actually buy the projects and turn them into co-ops.

An ethical and political nightmare, but with money, anything's possible.

It seems someone finally figured a way to get all that waterfront property out of the hands of the poor. I'd overheard a cop talking about it earlier in the locker room, "I stare at a wall from my apartment window while niggers are chillin' on welfare in beach front property!"

We'd never even thought of it as kids but for whatever reason our projects, like most projects in New York, were built on the waterfront.

A theory I heard on this explained how back when people were trying to figure where to put welfare housing for the poor, (where to hide us) they'd all agreed on the waterfront for two reasons:

1. It was cold as shit in the winter.
2. Subways were a mile away.

Back then I take it, nobody had cars and the middle class took the subway.

I guess somewhere along the lines of the middle class evaporating and the rich figuring out proper heating, someone noticed the magnificent views from Queens being blocked by those damn big ugly buildings.

So it seemed this new company figured there was a killing to be made buying the projects and turning them into waterfront condos. Makes sense I guess.

By enlisting, with I'm certain legal bribes of some sort, the 118 police precinct, they were gonna "smoke the residents out" by constantly harassing them until they couldn't take it any longer.

These same realtors had suddenly and coincidentally "invested" large amounts of funding into a new program started at the 118 called, the "Quality of Life" sweeps. Offering lots of overtime, a great new P.A.L. baseball field, and who knows what else?

We were indiscreetly "asked" to find a way to

distribute as many misdemeanors to the residents as possible, hopefully and eventually making them eligible for relocation. Who could have guessed how unpopular the serious offense of loitering was about to become there?

And whatever Good Samaritan "slipped through the cracks" would be met with the daily temptation of flyers posted on all their doors which read:

$10,000 to relocate!
WE'LL PAY FOR YOUR MOVE (CASH)!

Just to the right was a drawing of a happy couple holding all that cash in hand.

Sinister, greedy, opportunistic, genius and worst of all legal. And I get it: No one had to take it. But you tell that to the old lady dodging junkie bullets to cash in her food stamps.

And there I was, part of the plan to eliminate my old home and the people living in it.

Captain Mathers insisted Officer Prudenti and I go outside with him. Take a walk. Away from the madness. Out on the street, he placed the latest article from *The Gazette* into my hands. A new one. He asked me to look at it. Insisted on it.

He took his time, salivating as I read every bit of it—a

sadistic pleasure in watching me squirm. And right on the page it was folded to was all the proof I needed. The latest letter.

In the same almost scribble-type writing it went on about how they were going to expose the people involved in the cover up back in 1986 if the cops didn't "stop fucking with the residents." Stop the bullshit "Quality Of Life" sweeps!

The letter went on to explain how the two murders were not going to go unnoticed any longer. That the 118 had covered them up all those years ago. How these letters would breathe new life into the unsolved case.

That the two "murdered nobody's" the 118 deemed unworthy of a proper investigation were going to finally get their day, their headline, if the police did not stop their harassment.

Mathers looked right at me as he gave us the orders: "I want you two to go over to that reporter, Loren Bridges. The idiot who's printing this shit and remind her she's not hunting the Son Of Sam here OK? Remind her we're fighting a war on terror in this fucking city already."

MATHERS

And, nothing crazy but... I'm
getting a lot of shit about making
the neighborhood seem nicer so
these high rise investor fucks
can come run us all out of here.
You understand?

Like a good obedient dog, Prudenti, half listening, said
we'd be right on it.

Mathers then turned to me. Confirming my worst fear.

MATHERS (CONT'D)

Last thing any of us needs is
them reopening some unsolved
16-year-old case. None of us want
that I imagine.

And, with that, the gig was up. How much he knew or
where he was going with it, I couldn't be sure. But at
that moment, I remembered that old feeling. The one
that says, nothing from here on will be the same.

We pulled away. My eyes half on Mathers. His dead
set on mine.

On the drive over, Prudenti, as always, went on with his 9-11 conspiracy theories, the "still living" Bobby Kennedy, the inside on Pearl Harbor...

He'd ramble on and on while all I could think about was what Mathers' plan was. What did he want? How much did he know? Who was writing the letters?

In my paranoia I wondered if Prudenti was a part of it all?

I couldn't imagine he had anything to do with anything as he teetered back and forth, one part conspiracy theorist, other part, "twenty in, twenty out." So complicated in his simplicity.

I dared to tiptoe around the issue.

Trying to remain cool, I nonchalantly asked why Mathers cared so much about the articles. In half a daze he replied, "Fuck knows."

And in that I found solace. Peace in the idea that at least one person didn't give a shit about anything.

WE ARRIVED at *The Queens Gazette* office ten minutes later.

A dive sitting atop Rosarios Deli, across from the last stop on the elevated N train.

The sound of squealing subway brakes filled the unpleasant air of the tiny makeshift office.

My whole life was riding on the popularity of a newspaper no one even bothered to place lost dog ads in anymore. Either way, for me, this was life and death.

And there she sat, the reporter, Loren Bridges, alone. A one-time pretty mess hanging on to a crappy dated accent. In the midst of what looked like a sea of files. Files?! Who even has them anymore?

In two minutes I'd figured her to have been some gung ho, wide-eyed foreign exchange student who came, probably twenty years ago, in hopes of breaking a story for the *New York Times*; but instead, landed in the purgatory of a Queens local gazette hell, reporting on pizza places turning fifty years old.

The look on what I imagined her once opportunistic face was plain and simply the look of tired.

Once we questioned her about the articles though, she lit up. Like a rusty old neglected windup toy, way deep, buried... I sensed a tired spark.

There was no scarier look she could have given me; as I knew this was her moment. Her chance to do something, anything.

Whether the letters were real or not I figured it was a win-win situation for her. She was finally perking some interest and I was certain that, for her, that was more than enough. For the first time in years, imaginary or not she was actually being a reporter. Justifying her position. Her purpose.

At the very least, she was getting a response. More excitement than she'd had in years.

Looking around her office, her personal hell, there were glimpses of a rebel trapped in a neighborhood consumed with itself. I could only imagine her frustration. A previous headline confirmed it: "Taco Bell comes to Queens." Really? In all of the two minutes I'd been there I could hear her subconscious crying out about that type of work, "WHO GIVES A SHIT?"

On the walls it was as if she was holding her own personal demonstration against the 118. Like a DJ trapped at a Top 40 station playing Minor Threat at his lunch table, Loren Bridges was crying out for HELP on her walls. And the letters from MDC were quenching a thirst she'd almost grown to accept.

Everywhere you looked were claims citing the local 118 police department as corrupt. Rejected articles from her boss tying the Real Estate Developers to the 118's raids were taped anywhere a half-blank wall space could hold. In fact, Loren Bridges had the whole corrupt neighborhood nailed down to bumper sticker status and no one gave a shit but her.

I imagine the idea that someone was reaching out to her with information calling the 118 on some injustice was worth the backlash even if it didn't pan out.

I suddenly noticed a poster of Detective Stanford on the back wall. The detective from my youth. A photo of him side-by-side with Mathers. Comparing them as equally corrupt. It stated that Mathers was looking to replace Stanford as the new Deputy Police Commissioner. Somehow I knew that all meant something. That somehow this whole mess was connected.

She took notice of my observation. "You like that huh? I made it myself. Couple of monkeys." She said half under her breath in self-congratulatory disdain.

Then Prudenti fired right back: "Listen, stop printing the fucking letters. They're all bullshit and you're gonna come across as a fucking idiot if you don't!"

Wow, I thought. Well, that was straight. Must be the "twenty in, twenty out" Prudenti talking. The one that'll do whatever Master Mathers sends him to.

She smiled with defiance. Almost welcoming the challenge, and responded: "You know, every mafia wannabee in this neighborhood became a cop. Big facades with your 'hero' 9-11 charity bullshit."

To break the tension and get back to my own agenda I asked to see the letters.

She took them from her desk as Prudenti grabbed for them. Somewhere between kindergarten play and life and death she pulled them back.

"Tampered evidence is wasted evidence officer!"

He snatched them and let her know it "ain't evidence 'til someone gives a shit!"

The back and forth continued as all I could focus on was the fact that the letters were real! This was really happening. Someone was actually anonymously sending these. And whoever it was, knew I was guilty of murder.

I stared at the handwriting on them, scanning any memory I had of Vinny's but I was so consumed with fear it was simply one big blur.

If there was solace to find, (which there wasn't) it was in the fact I was pretty certain even Bridges didn't know how big a story she was sitting on.

Trying to mask my uneasiness I asked how many letters she'd received?

"Three, and from here on, the minute they come in, I'll print them."

She went on that the letters started right after Christmas. Very specifically she pointed out how they coincidentally started right after the 118 went in and arrested half the Queensbridge Projects on such heinous crimes as living below the poverty line.

When Prudenti chimed in with a wisecrack she quickly asked whatever became of the woman who'd filed excessive force charges against him.

The back and forth banter between Prudenti and Bridges sounded like two people overly familiar with each other. A hostile old married couple with too much knowledge of each other's buttons. A neighborhood version of Who's Afraid of Virginia Wolf.

Through it though, a clearer picture was beginning to emerge. I tried to present myself as simply a spectator when what I was doing was analyzing every last word.

Bridges then turned to me...

BRIDGES (CONT'D)
You see Officer, and I'm sure
you've been briefed, there's a
strong campaign coming from your
118 to rid this neighborhood of
impoverished undesirables and a
few of us still find something wrong
with that. How about you?

It was uncomfortable the way she continued to talk,
somewhat interrogatively to me. I guessed, or hoped,
she's figured there'd be no negotiating with Prudenti so
I was her best bet. And unfortunately she was right, but
for all the wrong reasons.

BRIDGES (CONT'D)
I called your Captain Mathers
after I received the letters, he
could give a damn. Seems no one's
interested in the possibility
of police doing anything corrupt
since this whole 9/11 debacle.
Your "Quality Of Life." A bunch of
garbage.

Feeling exposed, somewhat naked in the room, I
looked to see if Prudenti was picking up on any of it.
I was quickly reminded how little he could give a shit
as I caught him enamored with a photoshopped poster
of Captain Mathers pissing on the city. The shit eating
grin on his face confirmed the "twenty in, twenty out"
Prudenti was still in full effect. Strangely, I began to
wonder if even Bridges meant what she was saying
anymore. Beaten down by years of disappointment, at
times it was as if she was reading from a mantra she'd
written long ago but no longer related to. An entire
neighborhood full of "who gives a fuck!" It's a wonder
the traffic light didn't just say, "Fuck it... green!" Through
it though, Bridges continued. And although it came
across like a pre-written script, she had no idea how on
the nose her assumptions were:

BRIDGES (CONT'D)

Minute the story came out it
seemed your real estate developers
didn't like the idea of all that
waterfront property they're
salivating over having any kind
of negative connotations. The hell
they could care about displacing

an entire community. But a corrupt
police force... that's bad for
business... bad for Commissioner
Stanford being he used to run
around these parts, and worse for
Mathers, licking his chops at the
thought of replacing that old piece
of garbage.

As she, once again, pointing out the connection
between Mathers and the detective from my youth I
looked at Prudenti who simply wanted to go home. And
so... he did. Just like that. Out the door. Fuck it.

Refusing to be shut out, Bridges then turned to her
last bit of audience, me.

BRIDGES (CONT'D)

You know, Officer, every time someone
wants to dismiss one of my articles
they go on about how no one reads
them. We have a circulation of over
100,000. You can tell me the last
time that many people knew a cop for
a good reason?

Preoccupied with the correlation between Mathers and old Detective Charlie Stanford I had no answer. And nor did she want one.

She then asked me to leave.

I spent the next good minute on the steps outside her office tuning out the loud screeches of the train plowing by.

What I gathered is... the 118, under orders of "cleaning up the projects" by the Real Estate Developers, pissed off someone who knows what I'd done all those years ago.

Mathers wants the letters to stop. Stanford must had confided in him about what I'd done all those years ago and I imagine they either think it's me sending them or I must know who is and can stop them myself.

MEMORY IS
STRANGE.

Fragmented at best. Bits and pieces of what we choose, or what chooses to remain.

I recall a phone call all those years ago from Vinny. Before they'd put him back in that hospital.

He was rambling. Incoherent. Frightened.

I took the long extension cord from our wall-mounted dial phone into the bathroom with me.

Charlie, my faithful dog, stood guard outside.

Vinny was illegible if that term can even apply to speaking.

"Hello?"

"Milk, please don't hang up... please..." He'd said in the most desperate voice I'd ever heard.

Fifteen minutes prior to the call I'd gone looking for him. His mother didn't answer when I knocked but I heard her walking around in there.

She always played all sweet but I knew what she thought no one knew. The hell Vinny was in. The hell she chose to ignore.

It took me and Vin four full years of being together

night and day, having no one but each other for him
to tell me. And four years, at that time, were a third of
our lives.

He told me the terrible things her boyfriend said and
did to him. The threats.

People know, hear and see what they choose to
sometimes. But the black eyes. How could anyone even
pretend they weren't there?

My twelfth birthday Vinny showed up with his right eye
so closed there was no avoiding the conversation. Bad
as my situation was, no one ever hit me, at least no one
in my family. I guess I was only down to one member
so the odds were on my side. And, although they say a
beating's a beating, I'm certain there's something a lot
worse about it coming from your own family; and even
worse when it's being allowed by someone in your family.

I remember the day he told me his story.

It was the first time anyone had ever talked to me
sincerely about anything.

We were in my room playing a Bad Brains record we
stole from the Record library up in Lincoln Center on one
of our magical escapes to Manhattan.

I looked at his closed blackened bloodshot eye. He
said he'd fallen down the stairs. I didn't believe it for a

minute. I actually thought he'd gotten into a fight and was embarrassed when suddenly he told me about his mother's boyfriend. How he'd done it.

I asked why and it was as if the flood gates had opened and as much horror as there was to be instilled in a twelve-year-old boy came flooding out. The beatings, the cigarette burns, the fear, the molestation... and that was only the beginning.

Seems it had been going on as far back as he could remember.

He went on for two straight hours about it.

At the end I didn't even know what to say so I said nothing.

He insisted I give some kind of reply but all I could finally muster was a twelve year old, "That's fucked up."

So on the day no one answered his door I went to the roof. He was always up there. We were.

It was our safe haven of random thrown away things we'd collected over the years. A punching bag, some weights, an archery set with rubber suction darts. Just a bunch of junk on a roof. But it was our place. Away from everything.

I walked cautiously up the steps hoping he'd be there. I had my reasons for being cautious. Murderous ones.

I saw the door opened a crack and peeked out to our nighttime sky.

Junky a place as it was, warm summer nights up there were breathtaking. Even for us.

The 59th Street Bridge separating Queens from Manhattan on the roof of 40-11 is a site you never forget. Huge, magnificent, full of secret agendas, but after this night... awful ones.

The cover of darkness previously was, for us, a chance to be boys. Talk about the future. Embarrassing things we couldn't say to anyone but each other.

We'd sit up there wondering what was across that river? All those normal looking houses. All those trees.

We'd go hours on hours making up scenarios about what each apartment light across that river had going on in it. Their families, their jobs, their mistresses. Even in the roughest winter nights it was always a welcome place. Shivering up there, but together, away from everyone.

This night would change all that, as I creaked open the door...

Vinny's mother's boyfriend was unzipping his pants.

Even though I'd heard the stories, I hadn't seen it. And they are two very different things.

I couldn't believe it.

Suddenly, the slightest crackle from the door caused Vinny to look and see me.

It's old and cliché but his eyes and mine were saying a million things. Frozen. In disbelief of our helplessness.

We just stared at each other as that fucker did his thing. No idea I was there. No idea I could have grabbed a kitchen knife and rammed it right into his fucking back. But I didn't.

Instead, I did nothing.

I stood and stared at my friend and did nothing. The friend that never thought twice to do whatever it took to help me.

His eyes welled up with apologetic rage. It was as if he was saying he was sorry for letting me down, ME!? Not being man enough to say, "Get your stinking body the fuck off!"

I couldn't take it any longer so... I left. Left him with his own demon. Fuck, I thought. I got enough of my own.

DOWN THE STAIRS

I thought how wrong it was to leave him up there. He'd have never done that to me. I was ashamed beyond words but in the end... I still left.

I got to my door and reached for my key when suddenly right behind me was Geronimo. The last person on earth I wanted to see.

I knew he had my gun. The gun I stole from the man I killed.

I knew he knew something... I wasn't sure how much. But he certainly did know something.

On instinct I looked for Vinny, but this time he wasn't coming. He was busy being molested on our roof.

> **GERONIMO**
> What up Milk? Damn, you kids are
> cold. Killing junkies, partying and
> shit afterwards. Fat Vinny up there
> sucking his mama's boyfriend's
> dick. Fuck is that about?

I told him we didn't kill anyone. That Hanky O.D.'ed in
my apartment. He laughed at my attempt.

> **GERONIMO (CONT'D)**
> O.D.'ed? Fucker musta' slipped on a
> gun, jumped into your bathtub for
> one last cleaning. Cuz we know how
> strong he was about being clean.
> Gun went off. Yeah I could see
> that.

He then pulled out the gun. The evidence. The thing
that could ruin my life.

> **GERONIMO (CONT'D)**
> Don't worry I mean, Hanky was a no
> good junkie anyways. Junkie with a

```
three hundred dollar debt and a gun
just like this missing when I try
to put the pieces together. Pieces
of a fucking murder.
```

He kept staring, reading me with his acne-riddled face...

He then took the gun and pointed it right in my face and let me know the deal. I was to get him $300 and I could have my gun back. An insurmountable number at the time.

As he left the only thing I knew for certain was that certainly was the gun. How could I ever forget that awful smell of firecrackers?

WHEN I GOT INTO MY APARTMENT, the phone rang.

In that bathroom on my long extension phone cord I listened to a panicked Vinny, "Milk, please don't hang up. Please! You know I wasn't gonna do anything."

I told him I didn't see anything on the roof as I tugged on the cord to get more leeway.

He asked if I thought he was a faggot. I said, no.

Then, with what must have been the hardest thing he'd ever found a way to say, he asked if I was still his friend.

Of course.

In looking back, remembering, it dawns on me how once again, for him, it was all about me... us.

More afraid of what I might think of him. That he may not remain in the same light. That in some way maybe he had let me down.

The fear of losing his friend far outweighed the horror he was enduring. And if I am to be truthful... all earned.

At the time I didn't know what he meant. I knew he didn't want to be there but it was all just... confusing.

As an adult it's so much clearer. As a child you go with your instincts and then later on, sometimes, you understand them.

To me, I believe it was the idea that Vinny didn't want to be there that scared me most. That someone could force him to do something he didn't want to do. If he couldn't protect himself how could he protect me?

A long minute of silence over the phone followed until he told me he knew where his mother's boyfriend hid some money. That he had over a thousand dollars stuffed behind his couch in his red apartment. Although he always stayed at Vinny's mother's apartment, the boyfriend had his own on the fifth floor which he appropriately painted blood red.

It was "time" according to Vinny. Time we left the place we both hated. His last ditch attempt to keep us together.

"I hate it here, Milk... I hate it so fucking much."

All I could manage was a mousy, "Me too."

The plan was we were gonna break into that apartment the next day when we knew he'd be at the unemployment office. We'd take the money and be gone. Two fourteen year olds and a thousand dollars.

BACK IN STATEN ISLAND,

I laid on my cozy bed beside my wife and daughter thinking about that plan we had all those years ago. Me. Vinny and that thousand dollars.

The parallels sixteen years later were mind blowing. Everything was once again unraveling. I had everything to lose now, just as I did then.

The next morning I walked back into that insane asylum. The 118.

The "Quality Of Life" sweeps were becoming more obviously a corralling of the underprivileged. Growing by the day. A job maliciously well done.

Even Prudenti was becoming uncomfortable with it I thought as I watched him hand one kid a cup of water. Strange to see he had a human side.

A tranny was busy screaming at a cop about what we were up to. She seemed to have it all figured out. "You fuckers getting kickbacks to get warrants to kick us outta those damn projects! Think I ain't aware of your shit!?"

I'm watching her spewing the truth as... Mathers calls us into his office.

He closes the door with that look. Peripheral vision of a lizard. He takes his time as he always did.

It's obvious, he likes the power, likes to see people squirm. Imagine *SAW 3* in a police station, but real. Whatever it is he's trying to accomplish, he is. And like everyone in his presence, I'm squirming.

MATHERS

Jonathan, someone went in and tore
The Gazette's office to shit around
11 p.m. last night. I know Bridges
15 years. If you think you're gonna
keep her quiet like that you'd be
better served putting two bullets
to the back of her head.

I tell him I had no part in that. He smiles to let me
know he's just fucking with me. To remind me this whole
place is one giant mind fuck.

He then tells me and Prudenti to head over to the
paper's office and tell the reporter to "let us do the
police work from here out."

The good soldier and half-listener Prudenti tells him
we're on our way. I look over to notice him playing with
a squeak toy. Some kind of monkey thing or something.
Once again, that comforting reminder that he, as always,
could give a shit.

WE ARRIVE back at *The Queens Gazette* office fifteen minutes later. It's a mess. The Loren Bridges I'd met earlier seems a bit more unhinged. Less defiant. Prudenti smells blood and goes for it.

"Told you, you shouldn't be fucking with shit no one cares about."

He's gone too far. Not knowing how to simply sit on his hand he breathed new life into her.

"Really?" She perks up. "And you think this will stop me from printing these letters?"

I assure her we had nothing to do with what happened to her office.

Not one for politics, Prudenti tells her to fuck off and leaves.

In her vulnerable moment I see my chance, my moment to exploit it. But what can I say?

I asked if she had any idea who was sending the letters.

Her blunt, simple and horrifying answer was, "it doesn't matter," as she handed me the latest copy of her newspaper. The one just released.

"Go ahead, take a look," she insisted.

I did.

Loren Bridges,
No one cares but you.

The police continue to attack us.

Next letter I'll give you the two pig cop
names who covered up the murders
of Henry "Hanky" Williams and
Terence "Geronimo" Davis and
then everyone will care!
—MDC

MY NIGHTMARE.

She tells me she's looked up the names suggested in the letter and finds them to actually be two unsolved homicides.

She's getting closer.

I look back to be sure Prudenti's gone and in that instant realize maybe he's exactly what I need. I'm seeking the least of my enemies and at this point, stopping the letters at any cost may be my only chance.

"Mrs. Bridges?" I say. She corrects me that she isn't married.

"Ms."

"Yes?" she replies before I can finish. My train of thought now lost.

Like the cat who's eyed her canary, once again, out from the rubble, she emerges on top.

With my train of thought lost, she offers, "You know, you can't just be a cop Mr. White. Eventually you become one."

Not sure what she means, I uncomfortably force an insincere smile.

She looks again, more observantly, then adds, "Those clowns you work for, you don't seem like one of them.

But eventually, you will. You'll just do your job. Ask no questions like that moron who just walked out. Become another of that blue mafia."

I take that to mean she still doesn't know what I'd done...

I feel the urge to leave. This situation is like a dirty apartment that I know will be there when I get back, but right now I gotta go. Gotta think. Get out. Take a breath. Hope it just goes away.

I SIT
WITH PRUDENTI in a Subway sandwich shop.

He asks what her latest article says. I tell him it's another letter. That in the next one the person says they're going to give the names of the cops. He takes a moment, "What about the murderer?" Before I can ask what he means he continues, "All this fucker's concerned with is the cops, what about whoever killed these people they're talking about?"

I don't know how to answer that but feel the need to try. "Probably all bullshit, right?"

He hesitates. A moment of concern or (he is not listening) and then he replies: "Fuck her."

I exhale. The good ol' "twenty in, twenty out" Prudenti.

In my moment of comfort I overplay my hand, "No one's reading or cares anyway, right?" I wait for a reaction.

He takes a moment. Then looks square at me. "No one, but you."

THAT NIGHT I drove by my old projects.

I pulled up on 41st Avenue and just stared.

Appropriately, it began to rain. And there they were: the castles. The ones with which I'd mythically entranced my daughter's imagination. The giant castles.

I sat there and looked up at the fourth floor. A random old light bulb that needed to be changed flickered in a dirty bathroom of some new sucker's apartment. I wondered if they hated that place as much as I did.

And it brought me back to that plan we had all those years ago. The plan that was gonna take us outta here. Me and Vinny.

IN 1986 I put my dog Charlie on a leash and headed to the fourth floor to meet Vinny. This was to be the day we left it all behind. All the shit in those projects.

"What are you doing with that dog?" He asked. I didn't have an answer. I just wanted to bring him. I don't know. The thought of leaving him behind just sounded terrible. I knew no one would take care of him.

In his nervous hushed tone he said we couldn't bring a dog where we were going. I reminded him we had no idea where we were going.

He paused and told me to tie Charlie to the stairwell. He had the key and we were gonna do this fast. Go into his mother's boyfriend's apartment, get the thousand dollars from behind the couch and be gone. Gone from it all. All this bad. "Go in and go out."

I tied Charlie to the banister as he opened the door and we went in.

The first thing I noticed was the blood red walls just as Vinny had described them. Hell.

Action figures adorned the jammed narrow side panels. A hoarder's nest. Shit was everywhere.

Vinny climbed and reached behind the couch. Charlie was barking from the hall.

"Go shut that dog up, Milk!" He said.

I turned to notice the door a hair open and then…
Geronimo appeared.

"Fuck you doing in here?

With all I had I pushed him out the door.

In the hallway Charlie continued to bark. I was stuck
between trying to quiet him and fending off Geronimo's
questions.

"You robbin' that homo's place? Better be in there
lookin' for my money if that's what you're doin'!"

Charlie continued to growl and nip at his leg.

Geronimo continued, "I'm serious little man, you
better be getting my money if you're in there robbin' that
faggot."

I kept begging Charlie to stop barking while trying to
keep Geronimo from getting in the door.

Suddenly Charlie got a grip on his ankle and must
have caught a nip onto his leg and Geronimo turned. His
attention and anger now fully on Charlie.

I was so afraid he'd hurt my dog I lunged at him which
threw Charlie into a rage.

Geronimo easily smashed me back against the door as
Charlie locked onto his ankle!

My good loyal friend Charlie, protecting me with all

he had. All a two-bit mutt terrier had until Geronimo suddenly turned and kicked him so hard he wrapped around the banister and crashed into the stairs.

He yelped at the end of his leash, then lay there, panting from his side.

I screamed and charged Geronimo again with all the hatred in the world. The more my dog yelped the more powerful I became. Charged with adrenaline, fear and hatred.

And there he went. Like it was happening a million miles an hour. Down the stairs he tumbled, just like in the movies.

And in that instance, Terence "Geronimo" Davis was dead. My second kill.

No longer did we have to find his three hundred dollars. But all that really mattered at this moment was Charlie.

Vinny came running into the hall as I held my dog, panting. Heavier and heavier, then quieter, then nothing. Charlie was dead in my arms. The pain was immediate and like nothing I'd ever felt. Ever.

From all the barking and yelling people started coming into the hall.

Vinny grabbed me and dead Charlie and rushed us up to the stairs. We hopped roof to roof, carrying my dead dog, then down the fire escape to 40th Avenue.

I was so sad and nauseous at one point I actually thought about falling off the fire escape. I didn't have the energy to jump but falling off in a half dizzy spell almost felt like the right thing to do. Just let it go.

Vinny would never allow that though. Strong and in charge he pulled me along.

I ran straight home and so did he. It wouldn't be until later that we realized we'd left the money behind.

AFTER OVER AN HOUR

AFTER OVER AN HOUR in that car, outside my old projects, remembering my old home, our old nightmares; the clock in my car read 9 p.m. and I was still an hour from Kerry and Charlie.

My cell rang and I hit silence. I started up my car and speeded off. The more things were coming together, the more they were falling apart.

I arrived home close to 11 p.m. A crash on the Verrazano Bridge made my bad timing worse. Kerry was awake but pretending to be asleep. That awful thing couples do.

Once the pretending stopped, she very frankly told me the doctors would be changing our daughter, Charlie's, medication.

Charlie was born with epilepsy. We'd been lucky that she didn't suffer from Grand Mal seizures (the worst kind) often and that the Dilantin she'd last been prescribed had kept even the smallest seizures pretty much at bay.

"What do they want to change it to?" I asked.

"They're going to try different ones until the seizures stop; trial and error."

Every year we go through this as her body becomes immune to the medication. Heartbreaking doesn't begin to describe watching your six-year-old daughter helplessly convulse as you wait to see which new medication will curb it. What will distance the seizures enough for you to once again begin to pretend they won't be back? "Harrowing" is closer.

Kerry asks where I was. Why I'm so late?

At the station, I tell her.

"You took that ridiculous police test so you could work right down the street and now you're two hours away and in no rush to come home. What's going on, Jonathan?"

I forcefully remind her I became a cop because we needed insurance and all those other things that come with having a baby and a normal life. That relocating me back to Queens was only temporary. That I had no say in the matter.

She knows there's more. The same way I do. We've been married seven years and I imagine the only way I've kept my secrets this long is by blocking them from my own consciousness. Not just for her or my family's sake but as is my theme—for my own.

People wonder how murderers or people who've done terrible things can just move on. The answer is simple:

survival. Same way we move on from the death of a loved one, a marriage gone wrong. We just do. And guilt, in real life or like sadness eventually just... subsides.

On this realization I couldn't help but wonder how Vinny'd dealt with it all these years. Was it all resurfacing now for him? Had too many years of a secret bottled up inside begun to wear at the seams? His seams. Was it time it came out? Time to confess? Nothing is forever I suppose.

Not even murder.

WITH A FAILED ROBBERY,

no money and less hope, Vinny and I found ourselves in our building's boiler room. We packed Charlie in a green garbage bag and put him in one of our A&P shopping carts. At this point Vinny was becoming more and more incoherent. He kept rambling how his mother was gonna freak out about what we'd done. That her boyfriend would know it was us who broke in. That there'd be serious consequences.

I was zeroed in on my dog, Charlie. I refused to throw him in the furnace or the garbage outside. He had been my best friend since I was born and, until Vinny came, my only friend. No way was he gonna be strewn across the garbage after all the late night pickers went through them for cans. And burning him sounded even worse.

We pushed my dead dog outside past the arriving police presence. Bigger than I'd expected for a junkie no one cared about. "Expendable" was the word Officer Charlie always used. But I guess a robbery attempt and a dead person (even if he was a junkie) did justify someone showing up.

The callousness of the police standing outside eating sandwiches and smoking cigarettes as Geronimo's lifeless body was being stuffed into an unmarked van was starting to make me wonder if anyone mattered to these people. It was as if inside the grounds of our projects everyone was expendable. Not that I felt bad for Geronimo. I didn't. Not for a minute. This was just simply an observation.

And there we were. Me and Vinny. Trying to give my dog a proper burial as the police tried to decipher a murder.

We made it to Rainey Park, which stood magnificently beneath the 59th Street Bridge. Charlie's last stop. Even though it was beside a giant dumpster I'd come to the conclusion this was a more dignified burial.

I couldn't even cry. I was dying inside but nothing came out. It was as if I was drying up.

Vinny tried hard as he could to strike up any kind of conversation but I was gone. Weird as he'd been, in my moment of need, his rambling stopped. I chalked it up to that superhero thing. Even in his own madness he knew I needed someone and there he was again.

In the far off distance a Little League game was being played. Funny how back then we used to think anyone in Little League must have been rich. I imagine it was a coping thing.

Blame it on the fact we couldn't afford uniforms, when all it really meant was someone cared. Someone somewhere took the time to pay whatever minimal fee it was or fill out an application for those kids and that was more than either of us had. Me or Vinny. All we had was each other and we both knew that was coming to an end. Or at least I did.

WE SAT UNDER THAT BRIDGE ALL DAY.

I couldn't bring myself to answer anything Vinny tried to engage in.

I remember making a moment of eye contact that he clung to like a lifeline.

I quickly looked away. Once again, afraid he might read into where my head was at now. Survival mode. Every kid for himself. I was gone. And he was to simply become collateral damage.

I'm sure he could tell. I could avoid the desperation in his eyes but not his voice.

He went on about how his mother was gonna surely put him back in that hospital. That there'd be a punishment for what we'd done and it was gonna be a stay at that psychiatric place.

I thought for a beat to tell him to tell her what her boyfriend had done to him but... I didn't.

"No matter what they do to me, no matter nothing

though, I'll never tell, Milk... ever. No matter what they do to me in that hospital. I'll never tell what we did. About Hanky or Geronimo. We'll always be together. And we're gonna be OK."

It was impossible to look at him. He was more scared of losing me while he would be away than anything they were gonna do to him in there. He wanted me to be certain that he'd never tell anyone I was responsible for the deaths.

But it was all too late. It was as if a plan had been written in my head already. It was time to go it alone.

I had an aunt in Staten Island who had promised to take me in. Who knows if she meant it? It was a long time ago and people say all kinds of things to little kids in funeral parlors. But I was gonna look into it. I had to get away.

Vinny kept going on about how his mother was gonna figure out that we tried to steal her boyfriend's money. That they'd put him back in that hospital for probably a month for "rehabilitation" or whatever they called it back then. But when he got out he was gonna get a job and we would get an apartment together. We'd be sixteen soon and then everything would be cool.

Young and scared as I was, I knew it'd never happen.

This time things were not going to be the same. Horrible as they'd been, it was even scarier knowing they were gonna change, but I just did.

FROM VINNY'S WORDS TO THE DEVIL'S MOUTH

he was in Elmwood Psychiatric in two days.

Incredible, the accommodations you can find on the state's dime.

My building was feeling like a place I no longer belonged. I'd had it in my head I was leaving. And there was no way that wasn't going to happen.

Even without Hanky or Geronimo around, my apartment was hell. Now, with Young Vicky not coming around anymore and Chinese James keeping himself on lockdown, it was lonely as well.

I'd called my aunt fifty times and finally got a return. She was gonna let me and my grandma come for a visit and "see how it goes." Like an obedient dog on death row I was gonna do whatever it took once I got there. Whatever it took.

I felt I had to see Vinny one last time. I wasn't gonna tell him I'd be gone when he got out but I wanted to see him.

I took the 7 train to Main Street Flushing and then the Q15A bus to what looked like a big ugly brick warehouse. Elmwood.

I went inside and sat across from my old friend. His hair was all afro'd out. Drool running down his chin, white shit on the corner of his mouth. I'd never seen him like that. Even as bad as things had ever gotten at home he was always clean. His hair was always done.

He kept staring at someone or something that wasn't there. Probably a light. And then finally, he spoke... mumbled.

At first I couldn't understand him. And then he repeated himself.

"We were summoned."

"What?" I asked.

"From the streets." He went on. "I don't know from where."

He kept repeating, "We were summoned, Milk!" He looked at me a curious moment, and then asked if I knew that poem.

Before I could answer he continued with more incoherent ramblings, "Laverne likes Pepsi in her milk."

"Laverne and Shirley?" I asked.

Anyone who tells you crazy isn't funny is either lying or

actually has been on the inside of a mental institution.

It's awkward and the best way I can describe it is, hard to believe. Someone tells you they broke an arm, you don't argue the fact. Same person tells you they're Jesus' son, you're sure they're kidding.

Like taking mushrooms, crazy is a slow burn. At first you'll "think" you noticed something. Over time you'll find out your suspicions were correct.

Crazy comes in slow waves it seems. Signs. Hints. And then one day you're there. Or your friend is.

"We were summoned," he went on again.

I kept thinking how I didn't want to be there anymore. The same way I didn't want to live in that building anymore. Or see any of those people anymore. A strange moment of angry clarity came over me.

I was mad at the guilt I was feeling. Not about the murders. Fuck those guys. But abandoning Vinny had been harder than I'd anticipated and I was mad at him about it. Mad I'd have to start this crappy life all over again. With a bunch of people I didn't even know.

I got up as he muttered more incoherent ramblings and I left. I left him for good.

THEY'RE
LOADING UP
AN EXTRA LONG
AMOUNT
OF FILM for the next long take in this movie.
Ray Liotta is fixing his collar. He looks so much like
Captain Mathers from the 118 it's terrifying.

Everyone's laughing about something, including Ray,
so I smile in compliance but he's scaring the hell out
of me.

I'm watching him go over his lines under his breath.
He doesn't think anyone's listening but they gave me a
headset.

                    MATHERS
        Funny whoever's sending these
        bullshit letters seems to be
        interested in everyone except
        the actual fucking killers.

The actor, Channing Tatum, looks at him defiantly in their private rehearsal.

From behind the film crew I stare at the monitor, remembering how I never had the bravado Channing's showing, but for the movie's sake it's probably good. No one wants the lead to be a pussy.

> **MATHERS (CONT'D)**
> It's time this shit stopped, don't you think?

Liotta could look no more like Mathers than if he'd played himself in this movie.

> **MATHERS (CONT'D)**
> This next article comes out naming names, all of us'll be fucked. But you? Your life'll be destroyed. Yours and your families. Obliterated. Do you understand what I'm saying?

I remembered thinking of killing him in that moment. Unconsciously touching my gun. It didn't matter that we were in a police station.

He laughed at my unconscious defiance. The fucker's perception was remarkable.

He then looked me square in the eye and said I'd have to find a way to stop the next letter. The one promising to name the detective who had covered up for me all those years ago.

Quite clearly he let me know he was slated to replace the previous Deputy Commissioner, Charlie Stanford, and if a letter arrived stating Stanford had been involved in a cover up it would ruin everything. And if it did, he would see to it that no one would fall harder than me.

Basically, if it got printed, I was going down and that was why I was transferred to my old neighborhood precinct. I had been meticulously brought in to either be executed or executioner.

IN
1986, after visiting Vinny in that hospital I came home to Detective Charlie Stanford sitting in my living room. He told me my grandmother had gone for a walk. He insisted I sit across from him on the couch.

He did it in the way he always did things: where passive aggressive meets straight-up threat.

"I'd like you to sit down, Jonathan. I want you to sit down right here, right across from me, where I can look at you. That OK?"

I did.

"I heard about your dog, Jonathan, nothing quite as painful in the world as that."

I wondered if he had any idea what kind of pain it was to lose the most important thing in your life.

We both knew where this was going even though I wasn't convinced he actually knew the extent of my involvement yet.

He half apologized in his insincere way for having pranced me around in front of half the neighborhood to question me about Hanky's death.

He said it wasn't right that he'd put me in harm's way to prove a point.

His apology made it worse. Knowing it was premeditated made me hate him even more.

I actually thought he just wanted to go outside that day. But Detective Charlie, as I would come to learn, always had a plan.

He explained how after my father died he felt an obligation to watch out for me but there was only so much he could do.

He told me what I already knew: One murder had now become two. That neighbor's had reported yelling, a dog barking, a yelp and then, silence. That, in the hallway, along with Geronimo's dead body, they'd found traces of a dog's blood but no dog.

He went on about how my grandmother had just told him how Charlie had just coincidentally passed.

He then took out Hanky's gun and told me he'd found it in Geronimo's pocket.

He asked if I recognized it. I didn't answer.

He took a long moment and insisted I look at him. "I want you to look at me when I'm talking to you."

I tried but it was impossible.

He told me how hard he knew I had it there. "These junkie's come and terrorize you. If I'm gonna speculate, I'm gonna think they hurt your dog and you got excited.

And I wouldn't blame you in the least. I'd have killed him as well."

He looked again and said how Little Vicky upstairs was living in a house of horrors. That he knew what went on with her. He'd had the calls from Child Services. That he heard Little Vinny was hearing voices from his mother's boyfriend and that's why they had to hospitalize him again. He knew everything that went on in our building.

He told me he couldn't save the world; that his badge didn't give him super powers.

He looked at me one last time. Clear through to my very soul and let me know in no uncertain terms how he was going to let me off. Let me get away with murder. That he sympathized with what it must had been like to be the only white kid amongst all these "animals." Rice in a raisin bin. That my father should have provided better. That the city should have. That it wasn't my fault what this place had done to me. He asked if I understood the magnitude of what he was about to do for me. I didn't.

He wanted me to answer so I did. Anything to have him leave.

He turned one last time to say he'd now done all he could. That this would be it.

That this would be the last time we would meet as man to child, and how a man had to learn to "live with shit."

He seldom cursed but I imagine felt the need for harsher words.

One more look and that was it. He put the gun away and left.

And for the next sixteen years of my life, it never happened. All the bad I'd done—gone. Buried in that special place secrets go. Secrets cops know how to strategically place.

Until now.

AT HOME my wife wants to know what's happening. At the precinct I've been told to make the letters stop. At the local paper, Loren Bridges can't wait to print the next one... so I go back. Back to where it all started: to see Vinny. Now.

I TOOK OFF MY POLICE UNIFORM and put on my real clothes and headed to the Queensbridge Projects.

It would have probably been a lot more sentimental if I hadn't returned previously in riot gear but life often gets in the way of sentimental notions.

I walk by a few teenagers sitting on those same old rusty metal dinosaurs (Hepatitis Rex). The ones I'd run past as a kid on my way to the supermarket. Drinking 40s, smoking pot. Some things never change, I thought as they greeted me in unison: "Hello, Officer." Letting me know, they knew what I was.

I took a minute to tell them I'd grown up here. They couldn't care less. "Doesn't mean you ain't a cop."

I entered 40-11 and there I was. Fourteen again. Incredible how home is always home. Even when it's hell.

Everything seemed so small. Somehow a dirty old stuffed animal wedged deep between a pipe and the collapsing ceiling was still there. Unbelievable.

I could smell everything everyone was cooking in the

entire building and with that, memories came flooding back. I took a moment and looked at my old door: 1C.

Up the stairs, tin foil, crack vials and misspelled childish graffiti were now replaced simply with... neglect.

On the fourth floor I looked at Vinny's door. Strange how all I could conjure up were feelings of emptiness. It simply felt... lonely.

Deep under layers of paint, I noticed an old sticker, still there on his door. WKTU. On the wall were the words "roof access" with an arrow pointing up. Instead of knocking I followed the arrow to the squeaky roof.

I stopped at the top step as I heard a dying battery operated tape deck playing a wobbly cassette of an old hardcore song. I stood at the squeaky door a long moment to listen: "I can't believe it's come to this... no place to piss!"

The band is MDC. Millions of Dead Cops. The initials the person sending the letters is signing.

I take a long minute and sit there daydreaming, if that term can apply. In this dream, I confront Vinny and he agrees, yes, he'll stop the letters. Loren Bridges at *The Gazette* wonders why they've stopped. Weeks go by and then... it's over. As if it never happened.

But if I'd learned from anywhere to leave your dreams behind, it was in these buildings.

I TOOK
A
DEEP
BREATH and walked out onto our old roof to the sounds of Millions of Dead Cops.

And right there, in our old spot, I saw Vinny.

I didn't know what to say.

The massive bridge that I hadn't seen from this view in forever, along with the old familiar sounds of far away car horns, all just took me over a minute. I lost my train of thought. Just went blank.

I looked for the words but how do you start a conversation with someone you haven't seen in sixteen years when it comes with such an agenda?

Suddenly he shut off his tape recorder and stared blankly ahead. Not interested in who I was, who just walked onto the roof. Nothing. Just blank.

I greeted him in that uncomfortable way time forces us to, when reacquainting with a person of such importance.

He didn't respond.

"It's me, Jonathan." I said.

Expecting recognition or at least something, Vinny
barely missed a beat.

      VINNY
You look good I guess, right?
That's good.

Then, with as much nostalgia as he seemed capable
of giving I heard him barely mutter to himself, "Milk."
It was as if deeply buried, a voice was trying to remind
him of who I was. Who we were. The moment quickly
passed as he picked up his 40...

      VINNY (CONT'D)
You want some?

I didn't. He then went on to ramble about things I
could barely understand. Mixed into it were tidbits of our
past. Hints about what became of us all. I picked up that
Chinese James had died.

      VINNY (CONT'D)
He wasn't a faggot though.
(Motions to his veins.) Drugs...

Poor James. Good kid. But it all felt like someone else's memories now. I was too preoccupied with the strange delivery of his lines. Like an actor bored with a script. He was just talking. Not to anyone in particular. As if he was simply stating facts.

And then, just like that, he got up and headed toward the roof door to leave.

I grabbed his arm and told him that we needed to talk.

In desperation I told him I had a wife and a little girl and that I didn't want it all destroyed.

For a minute it was as if I penetrated through that haze as he paused. An even more confused look came over him and then, for the first time we briefly made eye contact.

> **VINNY (CONT'D)**
> You have a wife and a family now.
> That's good. I always knew you'd
> be good. You'd be OK. That makes me
> feel good. But I'm gonna go now.

As he walked away I wanted to tell him that if he didn't stop the letters he was going to destroy both our lives when what I really meant was he was going to destroy mine. His already seemed pretty bad. What a phony. Just like the last time we sat under that bridge.

But all I could do was watch him leave. Out the squeaky door.

And there I stood beside his junky old tape recorder as I notice an old sticker on it: Millions of Dead Cops.

I PULLED in front of *The Gazette's* office on 31st Street.

I must have sat there for at least an hour. Not knowing why or what I was waiting for but I did. Pathetic? Sure. Desperate? Definitely. Just watching the deserted nighttime Astoria Queens street air when suddenly I spotted Bridges headed back to her office.

I rushed over, begged her to talk with me a minute... anything. "How about just a coffee? Five minutes?"

She took a second. "OK."

When I think back now I don't know how on earth it never occurred to her that the letters could be about me.

So caught up with her desire to take down the 118, like the person writing them, the murderer had become secondary.

Bridges and I took a seat in Mike's Diner on 31st Street, right below the elevated train. Everything connected with Bridges included the sounds of the subway overhead.

She ordered a coffee as I nervously nursed water.

First thing she said was how she understood I was sent by Captain Mathers. I told her this had nothing to do with him. That I was there on my own.

At the time I was so consumed with the need for someone to help stop this I didn't even think that the more I questioned the more I would become a suspect. But I'd gone beyond caring about those kind of things.

Before I could push any farther she smiled and pulled something out of a folder. It was her column for the upcoming edition.

She sat there, gushing over it. Told me to have a read. From her eyes, I could tell this was it.

> *The detective who covered up the 1986 Queensbridge murders was DETECTIVE CHARLES STANFORD!*
> —MDC

IN THE STRANGEST WAY,

I was almost relieved. As if words that hadn't been spoken in a lifetime were being yelled aloud.

At least the waiting would be over. The impending doom I always knew would one day surface was now in print.

The fact that she didn't immediately know this was personal, further proved my notion that she was overly focused on the demise of Mathers and the 118.

I asked when she was going to release it.

"Saturday is going to be a huge day," she cattily responded.

I blurted out that she couldn't do it. That she couldn't release that article. That... she shouldn't.

She smiled, "And why on earth wouldn't I want to topple those fuckers?"

I certainly had the answer, but it wasn't one I could offer.

She looked at me with a dime store detective's eyes, "You look like you've seen a ghost Mr. White."

Precisely, I thought.

"Please, Ms. Bridges, can you give me a week?"

Not that I had any idea what a week would do for me but... time just felt... safer.

She looked clearly at me in an almost caring way and responded, "If I were you, I'd stay clear as I could from Mathers. He's going down and he's going to drag everyone right along with him."

I couldn't have said it any better myself. As a matter of fact, Mather's himself had voiced that same sentiment to me earlier.

She sipped the last of her coffee and got up to leave. "You should be happy Mr. White. Two murdered nobody's from the projects you grew up in are about to finally get the justice they deserve."

We stayed a long moment on each other. It almost felt in that moment like it finally dawned on her that I'd grown up in the same place the murders had taken place. How I was the one who kept asking about them. How I was the one who kept coming around.

Did she figure it out right there?

I thought to just tell her: "It was ME! It was me and you're going to destroy ME with this!"

But I didn't.

She held my gaze an almost clarifying beat, which

quickly subsided once again into her hatred for the 118. And she left.

Through Mikes Diner's window, I watched her walk down the now deserted nighttime Queens street. My thoughts, all dark. All bad.

THAT NIGHT I drove back to my old courtyard. Where we dumped Hanky all those years ago. Right there, in a pile of smelly garbage.

I can still hear Chinese James making those dumb jokes. Lightening up the mood. If the mood of a childhood murder can, in fact, be lightened.

I can't help but wonder what would have been different if I'd just been caught back then. Imprisoned. What would I have served? Eight years? Maybe less. It would all have been long over by now.

It's not as if I'd done anything meaningful over those years, except for Kerry and Charolette.

I'm trying to understand why I'm here. I guess the old cliché rings true. We all return. Like a guilt magnet of sorts. As if summoned by legitimacy.

As opposed to being with my family I just stand here, beside the smelly old garbage riddled with my moral forensics.

How ridiculous to have thought the garbage in front of the building we lived in would be a safe cover for murder. But after all, we were kids. Not an excuse, just logistics.

I went inside once again.

On the roof, again I found Vinny. Standing by the edge.

Looking out at all that nothing we used to dream about it. A river, some construction... Roosevelt Island.

On impulse I felt for my gun. I don't even know why. I wasn't gonna kill him. And even if I were, what good was it gonna do?

It was all too late. There was nothing left I could do. The article was coming out in a few days exposing me to the world. My family.

I approached Vinny and tried to talk but once again it was too late. And there I was, all those years later, still looking for comfort from my old hero.

He continued to stare. I remembered that look. As a kid it'd be attached to long-winded talks of things we were going to do, places we were going to go... now, just a mystery I'd solved too late. It was Vinny, all the time. Writing those letters. Confessing for something he could no longer hold in. And along with that would come my own demise.

As I got closer he muttered about the time I saw him up on this same roof when we were kids. The time with his mother's boyfriend. The time he was being molested and I left him there.

Is this why he was doing this to me? Before I could answer, or ask, he wanted to know why I'd never told anyone about what I saw back then.

As I stood without an answer, he hit me with something I never saw coming. He wanted to know if I never told anyone "because we were friends?" He took a long moment, looked straight at me with the clarity of that strong little boy I remembered, and asked if I was still his friend.

I didn't expect that. It was as if we were suddenly fourteen again. Me and my old friend.

Five minutes earlier I was contemplating murder; and now I had an overwhelming urge to grab him. Hold him. Tell him how much I'd missed him all those years. How he was all I ever had. How I'd never forgiven myself for just leaving. How I'd dreamt time and time again about us under this same bridge. Planning my escape as he rambled on about our future. The one we never had... together.

Instead, I took it as my moment to remind him, "Vinny, you promised you'd never tell anyone about what happened with the murders."

It was as if my confrontation threw him so far into those old troubled memories he simply turned to leave again.

"Please Vinny. You can't go!"

He looked at me one last time. "I always knew you were gonna be OK. I always did." His ramblings suddenly infuriated me. Just like at that hospital.

I felt for my gun again. But if I killed him what would it change?

He kept walking away, towards the squeaky old door and then... he was gone.

I stood there as the door closed.

Alone on my old roof. Our old roof. Desperate measures revert back to romantic notions as I imagined being arrested up there. Maybe people would understand then? Understand what? I almost said aloud. How fucked my childhood was?

Any way I looked at it, any way I tried to imagine an ending where my world didn't end, I came up short.

Suddenly, across the courtyard I saw Young Vicky. Older now but... right there. Same old window. We locked eyes. I could tell she recognized me, as I did her. But before I could take the proper time to dwell on it...

My cell rang. It was Mathers.

"Am I gonna have to talk to your wife to get this done?" Before I could answer, he continued, "If you can't pull the trigger on your retarded old friend then we're gonna have to pull it for you!" And with that, he hung up.

I burst down the six stories and called Kerry in a panic. "Kerry, do you know where my gun is?"

She took a moment, "Why?"

I yelled for her to get out my gun; that I'd be home in less than an hour.

"Johnny, you're scaring me. I'm calling the cops!"

I reminded her that she was on with a cop as I peeled away in my truck.

IT TOOK
ME
YEARS to even begin to decipher the stories I'd been told by half the neighborhood growing up.

Junkies just have a way of talking shit and getting high.

I always used to wonder how so many successful astronauts, scientists and inventors ended up on the milk crates in my living room smoking crack. It seems crack, poverty and bullshitting go hand in hand.

I'm sure it has to do with the need to blame someone or something for how and why we all ended up there. Can you imagine what a highly evolved ego it would take to admit you were on those milk crates because you simply hadn't done shit?

Lying to erase something though, can be much more deplorable.

I've heard people misuse the phrase, "not a day goes by" about their memory of a loved one gone, a romance lost; I imagine the saying is mostly a romantic notion. Surely days, even weeks, eventually must pass. This one though, never.

In all the years since these "incidents" there hasn't

been a mirror I haven't looked into wondering when
this would come out? I can go the noble route and say
it was my conscience when the truth all along was, it
was my fear.

My conscience can and has adapted to what I did.
I've falsely justified it fifty ways but my fear of paying the
debt is what I've stared at in every reflection of my life.
So maybe now, this time, it'll finally be over. Maybe this
could be a good thing—it all ending.

It's been a long, exhausting run.

I GET HOME

and Kerry wants to know what's going on. She got a phone call. The caller told her to ask me about the two murders in 1986. I told her to get out a gun. These kinds of things sort of insist on explanations.

What can I say, though? How do you tell your wife, the mother of your child, that you failed to mention you murdered two people when you were a kid and got away with it? It just didn't seem that important?

I can't look at her. She'll know. So I ask what else they said.

"Is that not enough?" she rightfully gasps.

It's at this moment I realize the extent of the lies. My betrayals. I take a deep breath and decide it's time.

"Kerry, I love you."

"Don't tell me you love me. Tell me what's going on," she fires back.

I suddenly feel this lightness. I'm ready to talk, to tell her, when suddenly... BANG!

We hear Charlie convulsing upstairs. That awful rattling. Her little arms are probably caught in the railing of her crib, banging helplessly against it.

We rush up the stairs. Kerry grabs her in one swoop motion as I stand there as always, helpless. Paralyzed. I'm sick with myself.

"It's OK baby, it's gonna be OK." Kerry soothes her until she finally concedes. The shaking stops. The crying slows as Kerry turns her gaze to me. The air is thick with anger, fear and questions.

We lay her down to sleep and I look at Kerry.

I hand her the paper Loren Bridges gave me in that diner.

"Read it." I tell her. "Read where it says a detective covered up two murders in 1986, in the Queensbridge Projects."

She hesitates, knowing this is going to be bad.

"It was me. The two murders that article is referring to were committed by me. I killed those people."

She looks blankly at me. There's no going back now.

Just to the side of Kerry, a breaking story is on the news. I see a photo of local *Queens Gazette* reporter, Loren Bridges.

My gaze draws hers as we both hear how Reporter Bridges was gunned down, execution style, in her office at approximately 9:15 p.m. No more than twenty minutes after I'd last seen her at the diner.

THE STORY OF MILK

The phone rings. It's Mathers. "Prudenti's outside of your house," he says.

I look from our second story window to see Prudenti standing beside a car out front. Mathers continues, "Get in the car with him and go where he says. This shit ends tonight."

I hang up and look at Kerry. She's confused, scared and pissed but Mathers is right, this shit needs to end tonight.

OUTSIDE

I TELL Prudenti I'll take my own car. The obedient dog
doesn't miss a beat and gets in mine with me.

We begin to drive past the long weeds and picturesque
ponds of Staten Island, towards the Verrazano Bridge.

I'm looking for conversation but it's useless. I can't
help but wonder what he knows. If he even cares. For
whatever reason, what they have planned for me is not
one of the things on my mind.

As we drive across that big long Verrazano Bridge I
remember crossing it for the first time with Kerry and
a load of furniture crammed into our junky old station
wagon. I remember laughing as a lamp fell out the
window. Even more vividly I recall catching a glimpse of
myself in the rearview mirror laughing and wondering
how I'd been so lucky to come into such good fortune.

We pass a sign: Welcome to Queens. Suddenly my
thoughts change to more rational, urgent ones. Survival.

Before I can attempt a conversation with Prudenti he
blurts out, as always half to himself, "That's fucked up
about that dyke, huh? Her dying and all. That fucking
reporter."

I look at him; I wanna say all the clichés from every cop movie, starting with, "You don't have to do this." I want to warn him of the consequences. Unfortunately, I don't know what they are for him.

He tells me to get on the Grand Central Parkway and exit near La Guardia airport.

We pull off into a 20-block stretch of abandoned, stripped down, stolen cars, surrounded by dumping grounds and stray dogs.

We head into a huge gated lot along the East River.

Last stop for scrap metal, outdated hospital equipment and un-recyclable plastics.

Prudenti points to a two-story office that looks like an abandoned meat packing warehouse.

I can see a hanging light bulb flickering from upstairs. Impending doom. It's clear, nothing good is happening here tonight.

He tells me to go inside.

What can I do but comply?

If there's an answer, it's in there. In the hanging light bulb building in a metal scrap yard, at night. If it all weren't so serious, it'd be comical.

I walk in and up the off-orange shag carpeted steps. The walls are lined with photographs of Little League baseball teams, the local church, bingo and the last neighborhood feast of Saint Anthony. Funny how all those good things, when lumped together, reek of corruption.

At the top step, Captain Mathers opens the door. I stop a moment. Not that I'm surprised to see him, but, seeing him signifies the end of this ordeal. I'd exhale if I weren't so wound up.

He says to come inside.

I do.

He's playing a tape-recorded song by Millions of Dead Cops, for my benefit, I'm sure.

The next thing I notice is a huge cork billboard. Tacked up on it are at least a dozen photographs of me, my wife, my daughter. Once again, for my benefit. Not that the urgency of this hasn't struck me, but seeing Charlie further reminds me of the stakes at hand.

Mathers shuts off the tape of MDC.

"You really used to listen to that shit?" He asks.

I just look at him. He sits and recommends I do, as well.

He looks across at me, tells me he'd been going insane trying every possible combination of names with the initials M.D.C. before coming across that band.

"It was a sticker I noticed on your retarded friend Vinny's tape recorder—up on that roof—that lead me to that crappy music."

He lifts up the cover of the MDC album he must have purchased. Joking, he comments on the name, Millions of Dead Cops. "Geez, and my mother use to worry about me liking Black Sabbath!"

I'm still quiet as I notice a photo of Loren Bridges on the table with a huge X through her face.

Mathers walks to a desk, returning with a handful of photographs of me and Bridges at the diner.

"Those photos were taken at 8:30 p.m., thirty minutes before she was found riddled with bullets." He looks at me as if I needed to be reminded that I'm in deep shit. "I imagine that'd be a tough thing to talk your way out of."

From out of nowhere a hand touches my shoulder. I instinctively grab for my gun. Prudenti grabs his and points it at me.

I turn to see Detective Charlie Stanford.

"PUT IT DOWN, TOMMY,"

Detective Charlie says, letting me and everyone in the room know he's still in charge. Still powerful.

"Do you recognize me, Jonathan?"

Of course I do. It seemed time had done nothing but add an occasional line or two.

He insists I sit down.

In all of two seconds I remember that power, the kind that buckles you; his very unique blend of sympathy, authority and fear.

With his arsenal of weapons, he pauses, then chooses: sympathy.

"Look at you, last I saw you, you were a boy and I was a man." He takes the extra beat almost as if on cue, "And look at me now."

It's as if Mathers and Prudenti have cleared the floor for the star to take center stage. The one to get it done.

What I do know is if they'd planned to kill me this would be over. The squirming though, I remember well. That sadistic bond he and Mathers seem to share.

He's doing everything a long-trained cop should do. Intimidate and comfort me at the same time. Good cop and bad cop all rolled into one. I understood these tactics much better now than when I was fourteen.

"There's nothing to be concerned with, Jonathan. This is a family matter between us. All of us."

Mathers can't control himself as he puts it all out there. How I'm sitting in that seat because I murdered two people in 1986 with my old friend Vinny. He continues what an ungrateful fuck I was for not taking Vinny out the day they told me about the letters. How I should have been kissing the ground Detective Charlie walked on for letting me off the hook all those years ago. How we both should have been. But at least Vinny had an excuse. He was a "retard."

Mathers went on and on. His words intentionally cutting like a knife.

I see old Detective Charlie's face, hating being upstaged. I'm looking for an in, an ally, maybe this is it. Maybe Mathers will piss him off enough that...? What? I don't even know. I'm desperate.

Mathers continues about how he wasn't going to let the good name of Detective Charlie go down, especially on the eve of his retirement. I stare at him, knowing this has much more to do with his own shit than any respect issue.

The movies love that word: "respect." People like him love the word as well, as long as it's pertaining to some kind of personal benefit. Bunch of hypocrites. Me being one as well, but at least I'm aware of it, if that matters for anything. Aware of my own unworthiness.

Mathers keeps going. I can't hear anymore. "Listen," I say, "I knew your Detective Charlie OK?"

He jumps all over it.

"Of course you did. And as you can see he's an old man now."

Stanford can't take it any longer. "Stop talking about me like I'm not in this fucking room." I relish the moment, hearing Stanford raise his voice at Mathers. But it gets me nowhere. A momentary personal triumph. A grin as the noose drops over me, but I'll take what I can get.

Mathers continues, reminding him and everyone in the room that a changing of the guard is beyond in effect.

Like an old episode of Batman, he proceeds to tell me everything. About how when Bridges got the first letter he could give a shit. But then, they kept coming.

Eventually he knew it had to be one of us.

At first they took a visit to Vinny but deemed him incapable. So they brought me back. He went on about how delighted they were to find that I'd become a cop. Made me easier to find, easier to track, easier to manipulate.

They put in a request for me to be transferred to the 118 under the guise of the "Quality of Life" program. Consensus was, if they had me in their clutches they'd either figure how to get me to stop writing them or lead them to whomever was doing it. They went on about how they watched me for the first two weeks and, nothing. They baited me with the letters and were as baffled by my reaction as I was with them.

At first, they'd given me the benefit of the doubt of being a person with a guilty conscience. Someone with a soul. A human with feelings of remorse, regret. Confessing for my past sins by writing the letters myself.

As it turns out, they overestimated my morals.

After following me to the roof the first time, they knew it was Vinny. They thought to just kill him, end it right there, but forensics today are not the forensics of 1986. They also feared that might somehow stir up those lost old morals of mine to come forward and start confessing myself. So they hedged their bets on me being able to get through to him. Make him stop.

I thought about my gun at my side as always, which quickly brought a smile from both Mathers and Stanford and a stare from Prudenti. A room full of bloodhounds.

Desperate times lead to desperate measures and here we all were... desperate.

The threats now simply subsided to assignment.

I was to return home to my wife, child and "all the things I never dreamed I'd have," rightfully put by Mathers distasteful tongue.

He went on about how they were going to let me walk and take the next two days off. "And on your long drive home you're gonna think about your wife, and your daughter's five-year-old face."

MATHERS

And when you get there you're gonna put them on that ferry or whatever it is you people do on days off there. And you're gonna think how lucky you are to have half the 118 working overtime so no one finds out you're a cold-blooded killer.

He spits out those last three words like fiery liquid at me: "Cold-blooded killer." As if the 2 percent cop that still existed somewhere deep in that corrupt opportunistic mass needed to have its say.

I stare at him. I wanna say I'm not a killer but who would I be saying it to this time? Myself? Why pretend anymore? They're handing me a pass. My second one. The one Stanford all those years ago said I'd never get again. A clean slate on a life of deception and all I have to do is walk out that door.

> **MATHERS (CONT'D)**
> And when you come back in on Wednesday you'll get your transfer back out to the land where DUIs are your biggest concern. And here in Queens, Jonathan, there'll be a small blurb at best in a little newspaper about a crazed fan named Vincent Carter, Vinny, who wrote letters to a lonely reporter, killed her and took himself out the next day. And life will go on Jonathan. The one you never dreamed you'd have.

The price is now Vinny's life. Forensics and all, they were in almost as deep as I was. Almost.

They'd already killed the reporter, they had photos of me sitting beside her (thirty minutes prior to her being murdered), and two very different ways to go with their investigation.

All I had to do was leave. They'd then kill Vinny, label it a suicide, pin the reporters murder on him and his "rambling nonsensical obsession" with her, and everything would once again, return to normal. A "normal" I'd already lived with for many years.

They told me once again to leave.

I took a moment on it, if, for nothing else, to not look like the embarrassing half man I've always been. Willing to go beyond selling him out this time. Bartering his life for a more worthy one, mine.

I asked what they were going to do to him as if it wasn't already made very clear. I was met with a smile.

"Just go, Jonathan," Mathers said.

I wanted to puke, more at my own patheticness, but I didn't. The self-loathing must have been seeping.

I stared. There was no way out. Even if I had guts. There was simply no way out.

So, I left.

ON MY LONG DRIVE BACK

from Queens to Staten Island, I was consumed with visions of my past. Our past.

Vinny, his molestation, our plans, our dreams, our long talks at night on that roof. And now, for all he'd done for me, I was leaving him to die.

Dangling from my rearview mirror is a picture of Charlie—a perfect excuse to allow something horrific to occur to someone else. Who would blame me?

I'll be safe and asleep in my comfy bed, beside her and Kerry when it goes down tonight. When they kill him. In our crappy old building. Probably on our old roof. And just like old Detective Charlie said tonight and all those years ago, no one will care. "Not a single fucking person."

Another crazy worthless nobody goes down in a hail of bullets or drugs or however they do it at the projects.

Having history on my side I know this will pass, as well. The awful truth is humans can and do live with sin. Regret. We have enormous coping skills. We find ways to justify almost anything.

Vinny will die while I sleep tonight in the comfort of my middle-income home in the suburbs.

Days, maybe even months will pass, but eventually, we'll be a family again. We'll eat, laugh, drink and be OK with it. Vinny's death will just be another secret buried deep amongst the others. "Shit" I'd learn to deal with as a man.

And this is how it would have ended if it weren't for two images I couldn't shake.

The last time we saw each other as children, when, in that Thorazine haze he forced out, "I'll never tell, Milk. I'll never let anyone get to you." Still faithful, even through all that medication.

And the other night, on our roof. When he had that same look, sixteen years later, when he wanted to know if I was still his friend.

I want to turn the car around. But if I do, I'll jeopardize the little I do have.

To try and shake the urge I look again at that picture of Charlie and...

GRAB
MY GUN and spin the car around.

I love you Kerry. I love you Charlie. But I can't let this happen. Not again. I couldn't possibly live with it again.

I speed back across the Verrazano, past the Welcome to Queens sign. Exit the highway and pull to the foot of the Queensbridge Projects: 40-11 40th Avenue.

With my gun in hand I bust into my old building.

Up the stairs past the ghosts, the smells, the new teenagers. All I can hear is that MDC song in my head. That loud guitar blasting and those lyrics suddenly making absolute sense.

Floor 1

I remember getting intimidated, busted at age 13 by the police.

I remember my friend being shot in the back for his first offense burglary.

Floor 2

I remember the police firing into crowds, killing children because they were the wrong color.

I remember the narcs in high school trying to set me up for a big fall.

Floor 3
I remember the police bringing dogs into my school sniffing away my rights.

Vinny's Floor
Because the police is the Klan is the Mafia. Because the police is the Klan is the Mafia. Because the police is the Klan is the Mafia!

I see Vinny's door has been busted open. I recognize the style. A police battering ram. They've already been here.
I look at that arrow, "Roof Access."
I run up as the song subsides. The closed steel door is muting whatever is happening on the other side and all I can hear is my breath. Here again. With my gun in my hand.
And... BAM!

I bust the door open as Mathers turns and shoots me!
BANG!
Mathers, surprised by me being there, about to murder

Vinny, instead turned and shot me to the ground. Bang!

As I lay there, blood filling my pants leg, he frantically turned back to Vinny.

On the ground, I looked at my gun and Prudenti kicked it away.

I then looked up and straight into Stanford's disappointed face. All my ghosts on one roof.

In his madness, Mathers let me know the gun he just shot me with was the one we'd used to kill Hanky all those years ago. Stanford had saved it and they'd planned to kill Vinny with it and lay it all out a suicide. I'd messed that plan up, big time.

He screamed what a stupid fucker I was. That I was going to have to pay the price along with Vinny for coming back.

With Prudenti holding his gun on me, I helplessly watched as Mathers literally chased Vinny to the edge of the roof.

I could see him thinking, using all those years of corrupt cop instincts to figure what to do, and like a true problem solver coming with about as good a last minute solution as imaginable. Have it look like Vinny killed me with his old gun, and then they'd make his own death, as previously planned, look like a suicide.

In his moment of madness, he grabbed Vinny.

"Look at you!" Mathers screamed in his face. "A nothing! While this fucker left you here to rot! You should be glad I'm gonna blow his fucking head off!"

In the chaos I looked to Stanford who simply seemed like a confused old man. If I didn't know what a tricky fuck he could be I'd have almost believed he felt bad for me.

Mathers then lifted his gun at me as Vinny screamed.

"No!"

He charged Mathers. A scuffle ensued and Mathers pulled the trigger. It popped in Vinny's hand but Vinny kept going. He wasn't going to let them get to me.

And then, a second BANG!

Everyone stood frozen a moment until...

Slowly, Mathers slid to the ground.

Vinny had somehow managed to get the gun and shoot him. How could I have ever doubted my old superhero?

In my moment of awe, I looked at Stanford reaching for his gun.

"No!" I screamed, knowing what he was going to do.

He took his gun out as I continued to scream.

And then... BANG BANG BANG... BANG!

I watched Vinny fall back as Stanford unloaded into

him. Once, twice, three times, and then off the roof with the fourth shot.

I ran to the edge too late. Too late for everything. I turned to Stanford as he pointed the gun at me now. That old smell of firecrackers was everywhere.

"You ruined my life," I told him.

"You take one more step you don't have a wife, Jonathan. You don't have a family. You don't have all the things I made sure you were able to have."

And what could I do? Anything other than obeying him meant my daughter would, just as I had, grow up without a father.

Stanford then laid it all out, the whole new plan.

"You came up here with us. This person, Black Male, 30ish, suspected of killing a local reporter, opens fire hitting both you and Captain Mathers. I take my gun out and that's what happened. Jonathan, do you understand me?"

I started walking towards the old squeaky roof door as Prudenti pulled his gun on me.

I continued to the door as Stanford told Prudenti to put his gun down. To let me go. That I could be "trusted to keep my mouth shut."

AS I STUMBLED DOWN THE STEPS

I saw Vinny's mother in the hall.

She dropped her shopping cart, noticing the blood trickling down my pants beside her broken door. She knew what this could mean.

I heard her screams of "Vinny!" as I continued down. "Fuck her," I thought. Her screams just made me angry and I didn't want to feel that at that moment.

The banister and walls kept me up, out the door and past those old metal dinosaurs, to where Vinny was on the ground.

Still breathing. How? Four bullets and four floors later, as if waiting for me one last time. As he always did. Superheroes do these things.

I got as close to him as I could. "It's OK, Vin, don't talk."

All those years he'd kept quiet and there I was once again telling him with his last breath to just go away. Not make a scene.

He kept trying though.

Blood and dirt were getting in the way but he was insistent.

And then, finally, with all he had left, came his last words. "I never told anyone, Milk. I never did. I'd never let anyone get to you."

And my heart was broken all over again. Every bit of it.

My friend, Vinny. Always making sure I was OK.

From far away I could hear that awful sound of sirens arriving too late to the projects. A sound I'd long forgotten.

But my friend Vinny was dead. My secret was now buried with him in an open casket beside the dinosaurs. The Hepatitis Rex.

His eyes wide open to the sky.

As a leaf fell from a nearby tree I followed his eye line to a third story window where our childhood friend Vicky sat watching us. Perched at her post. As she'd always been. Always watching everything.

At that moment it hit me. Could it have been her the whole time? Was she the one writing the letters? She was always there. Back when Hanky died, when Geronimo died, at the police raid...

Much as it mattered, it just didn't at the time.

A CROWD
SLOWLY
GATHERED. Another anonymous scene to consume

the locals over dinner. Another nobody. Vinny.

In the following days, the *New York Post* covered
the story of a hero captain gunned down by a crazed
obsessed suicidal fan.

Stanford was deemed a hero. I, an innocent rookie
caught in the cross fires, who nobly rejected the notion
of being singled out.

And life would go on, Jonathan. Just as promised.

DAYS AND MONTHS PASSED with no new letters. Dormant.

True to Stanford's words, I was back in the land where DUIs were my biggest problem. At the local station in Staten Island, enjoying lunches with Charlie and Kerry.

If there was happiness to be found it was in the notion that Vinny hadn't lied.

I hung on to the idea it was Vicky all along. That she was the one writing the letters. And with all the death attached to them she just decided to stop. Just an instinct or a hope. But I wanted my hero to have done that one last thing for me.

My friend, Vincent Carter. The kind you read about in books. The kind you see in the movies. The kind you wish you were lucky enough to have had in real life.

Writing is strange, like a song or maybe old vault. One of the only things you know when you do it is that no matter how many people will ever know it, read it or hear it that it'll be this moment you're looking to capture and attempting to preserve. No way of knowing if you'll be successful but you try, right?

So here's mine. With Vinny. The two of us out here on the great lawn of our projects. With every last thing he has left he looks up and...

"We were summoned, Milk. I don't know from where. Summoned to be together."

What a beautiful thing to say to someone.

www.ingramcontent.com/pod-product-compliance
Lightning Source LLC
Chambersburg PA
CBHW050729250626
47155CB00005B/1723